INSIDE THE ANCIENT WORLD

THE BRIDE FROM
THE SEA

INSIDE THE ANCIENT WORLD

THE BRIDE FROM THE SEA

An introduction to the study of Greek Mythology

JOHN SHARWOOD SMITH

Drawings by Jonathan Wolstenholme

MACMILLAN

To MIF and JWR in gratitude and admiration

First published 1973

Published by
MACMILLAN EDUCATION LTD
Basingstoke and London
The Macmillan Company of Australia Pty Ltd Melbourne
The Macmillan Company of Canada Ltd Toronto
St Martin's Press Inc New York

Companies and representatives
throughout the world

PRINTED PHOTOLITHO IN GREAT BRITAIN BY
EBENEZER BAYLIS AND SON LTD
THE TRINITY PRESS, WORCESTER, AND LONDON

Contents

Peleus struggling to hold Thetis, who has turned herself into a cuttlefish

List of Illustrations

IT is difficult to decide how a book on Greek Mythology is best illustrated. The myths are timeless but fashions change, in clothes, armour, vehicles and musical instruments. Many of Jonathan Wolstenholme's drawings of mythological incidents are based quite closely on Greek vase paintings of the fifth century B.C., but others represent his own interpretations.

Cover drawing: *Peleus being greeted by Thetis. A drawing of
part of the decoration on the Portland Vase, made by an
Italian artist of the seventeenth century (before the vase was
broken)*

*This and the diagram on pages 88 and 89 are reproduced by
courtesy of the Trustees of the British Museum*

Author's Note   Names are given in their Greek form except for those
which are so familiar in their Latin or anglicised form that they would
look tiresomely odd: e.g. Oedipus *not* Oidipous, Hecuba *not* Hekabe,
Priam *not* Priamos. For pronunciation, see index.

General Editor's Preface

To get *inside* the Ancient World is no easy task. What is easy is to idealise the Greeks and Romans, or else to endow them unconsciously with our own conventional beliefs and prejudices. The aim of this series is to illuminate selected aspects of Antiquity in such a way as to encourage the reader to form his own judgement, from the inside, on the ways of life, culture and attitudes that characterised the Greco-Roman world. Where suitable, the books draw widely on the writings (freshly translated) of ancient authors in order to convey information and to illustrate contemporary views.

The topics in the series have been chosen both for their intrinsic interest and because of their central importance for the student who wishes to see the civilisations of Greece and Rome in perspective. The close interaction of literature, art, thought and institutions reveals the Ancient World in its totality. The opportunity should thus arise for making comparisons not only within that world, between Athens and Sparta, or Athens and Rome, but also between the world of Antiquity and our own.

The title 'Classical Studies' (or 'Classical Civilisation') is featuring more and more frequently in school timetables and in the prospectuses of universities. In schools, the subject is now examined at Advanced Level as well as at O-Level and CSE. It is particularly for the latter courses that this new series has been designed; also as a helpful ancillary to the study of Latin and Greek in the sixth form and below. It is hoped that some of of the books will interest students of English and History at these levels and, in the case of the present volume, the non-specialist reader as well.

The authors, who are teachers in schools or universities, have each taken an aspect of the Ancient World. They have tried not to give a romanticised picture but to portray, as vividly as possible, the Greeks and the Romans as they really were.

In *The Bride from the Sea* John Sharwood Smith has used a well known story as a point of departure for an exploration of the Greek Myths as legends, as folk-tales and as 'pure myths'. In the chapter on legend he discusses the general question of the relationship between myth and history as well as the particular question of the historicity of the Trojan War. In another chapter he lightly touches on theories about the origins and functions of myth which appear in the works of Freud and Jung, and in anthropological studies which have appeared since Frazer. In the chapter on folk-tales there is a brief discussion of the echoes of Greek myths which appear in French fairy tales and in the collection of the Grimm brothers. An epilogue considers the reappearance of Greek mythological themes in many forms in the present century.

The bride of the title is Thetis, wife of Peleus and mother of Achilles, whose wedding was the scene of that unedifying but fatal contretemps between the goddesses which led to the siege and destruction of Troy. But before ever the wedding could take place Peleus had to capture his bride as she lay sleeping on the seashore, and prevent her at all costs from escaping back to her natural element: and in just this way the lovers of other beautiful creatures from the sea have had to capture their brides in tales told as far apart as Yorkshire and the Pacific Islands.

The book is designed to draw attention to the charm of the stories themselves – many of them are succinctly retold – as well as to the fascinating conjectures to which the pervasiveness of myth gives rise.

January 1973   MICHAEL GUNNINGHAM

I

Peleus and Thetis

The Wedding of Peleus and Thetis

NEREUS was a god of the sea: an old man with a long flowing beard, pale blue hair and the knowledge of many hidden things. It was from him that Herakles learnt how to obtain the golden apples of the Hesperides. He was kindly and gentle and never told a lie, but to avoid answering awkward questions he would change himself into many different shapes, just as the sea can change its appearance from day to day and hour to hour. He married the daughter of Okeanos, the river which flows round the world, and they had fifty daughters, sea-nymphs called Nereids, the most beautiful of whom was Thetis. Thetis also was gentle and wise, and endeared herself to the gods by many acts of kindness. The time came when Zeus, the ruler of gods and men, wanted to marry her; but Thetis was reluctant because Zeus was already married to his sister Hera, the patron goddess of Marriage. Hera had been foster-mother to Thetis, and Thetis had no wish to make her jealous.

In the end Zeus gave up the idea, having discovered an alarming prophecy. Thetis' son was fated to be more powerful than his father; so if Zeus did marry her, his son would inevitably overthrow his rule, just as Zeus had overthrown the rule of his father Kronos, and Kronos that of *his* father before him. If, on the other hand, she married a mortal, her son would merely be the bravest, strongest and swiftest of men. So Zeus arranged for her to be married to the most eligible mortal who could be found. This turned out to be Peleus, who was then living in a cave on Mount Pelion under the protection of the Centaur Cheiron.

Cheiron was told by Zeus to arrange the wedding, which would be attended by all the gods; but Cheiron realised that Thetis would resent the prospect of being the wife of a mortal, and would have to be captured. Furthermore this would be no easy task because she had inherited her father's ability to change into strange shapes.

So Cheiron instructed Peleus to hide on the seashore near the foot of Mount Pelion, and wait until she came out of the sea. This he did, and at about mid-day she appeared, together with her forty-nine sisters, all beautiful, all riding naked on the backs of dolphins. Soon they stretched themselves out along the seashore for their siesta. Peleus waited until they had fallen asleep, and then rushed to seize Thetis. The other forty-nine Nereids ran shrieking back into the sea, but Peleus held tightly on to Thetis, even when she changed into fire, water, a leopard, a sea-serpent, and finally into a cuttlefish – that octopus-like creature which evades its foes by squirting sepia, an inky fluid, at them.

Peleus hung on bravely, and at last Thetis yielded and agreed to marry him. The wedding took place in Cheiron's cave and all the gods attended, bringing precious gifts for the happy bridegroom. But no one had remembered to invite the goddess Eris (whose name means 'strife' or 'discord'). Deeply offended, she arrived uninvited and dropped at the feet of the goddesses a golden apple, labelled 'For the most beautiful'.

*   *   *

That is a version (there are others) of an episode from Greek mythology. The character of Thetis could also be thought of as an image of myth itself. Like Thetis, myth can appear charming, beautiful and comforting, but it can also appear ugly and frightening. Myth is full of fascination, but it takes many shapes, and final definition of its true nature has so far escaped the classical scholars, anthropologists, professors of comparative religion, prehistorians and psychoanalysts who study it. And the reward to the hero who masters myth? Success, perhaps, in unlocking some of the secrets of the human mind.

Threefold division

Scholars usually separate myths into three classes: legends, folk-tales and pure myths. However, it is very hard to be precise about these distinctions, and mythical stories often stray from one class into another. Certainly, very few of the surviving stories from Greek mythology can be neatly pigeon-holed in this way.

LEGENDS

These look like garbled history. They contain references to events which actually happened, but these events are usually distorted without any regard for what is humanly possible, or for the real nature of the events themselves; and the dimension of time is either topsy-turvy, or simply does not exist.

These contain magic, talking animals, clever trickery and neat revenges; also monsters, ogres, witches and other supernatural creatures. They are not concerned with the relations between men and gods, or connected with religious worship; and they are thought – rightly or wrongly – to have nothing much to say about the more serious aspects of human life, such as marriage, death, sin and guilt, or the obligations imposed by living in society instead of living, like the animals, in a state of nature.

Dick Whittington and King Arthur

A convenient illustration of the relationship of legend and folk-tale to historical fact is provided by two familiar heroes, the one of folk-tale, the other of legend: Dick Whittington and King Arthur.

Dick Whittington is a simple-minded orphan boy who comes to London expecting to find the streets paved with gold. They are not; and he nearly starves until he is given work by a rich and kindly merchant. He is bullied by the cook, and his only friends are the merchant's daughter, who is always kind to him, and a cat (which he has bought for one penny to kill the rats in his garret), to which *he* is always kind. The rich and kindly merchant invites all his servants to contribute money or goods to the ship he is sending to trade in foreign parts. Poor Dick has nothing to contribute except his cat, which he parts with most sorrowfully. Soon afterwards the bullying cook makes Dick so unhappy that he runs away. After walking to the foot of Highgate Hill he sits down on a milestone to rest, footsore and miserable: but there he hears the bells of Bow church ringing. They say to him, 'Turn again, Whittington, thrice Lord Mayor of London'.

So he goes back, and finds that the ship carrying his cat has been driven by storms into a port in Morocco ruled by a millionaire potentate who has never seen a cat before and is suffering from a plague of rats. The potentate has therefore bought Dick's puss in exchange for wealth beyond the dreams of avarice. So Dick is rich and marries the merchant's daughter and is elected Lord Mayor of London three times.

The good but simple-minded hero, the prophecy of the talking bells, the good fortune brought by an animal to which he has been kind, the marriage of a servant or apprentice to his master's daughter, are all typical themes of folk-tale and to be found in stories collected from every country in Europe. Some of these actually have the story of the cat that sells for a fortune – a story which, after all, merely makes the point that successful trade consists of buying cheaply where there is a surplus, and selling dear where there is scarcity and demand. Typical also is the story's lasting popularity. There was a statue of the cat erected outside Newgate gaol in the eighteenth century, and there has been a commemorative stone (now surmounted by a brand-new cat) on Highgate Hill since 1820: and the story is still good for the plot of a Christmas pantomime. None the less, the records confirm that there really was a Sir Richard Whittington, Lord Mayor of London in 1397, 1406 and 1419. So we have a folk-tale which has attached itself to a genuine historical person.

There is no such documentary evidence for King Arthur. Nevertheless, he can reasonably be considered a hero of legend because many of the stories about him are concerned with a conflict which must have actually taken place. This was the resistance of the Britons to the Saxons who invaded Britain after the departure of the Roman legions to defend the collapsing frontiers of the Roman Empire. This struggle left a deep impression on the traditions of the Britons who survived in the mountains and forests of Wales, and in Cornwall and Brittany: it is from Wales and Brittany that the Arthurian stories originate, and some of them are located in Cornwall.

PURE MYTHS

This classification is usually reserved for stories which are directly related to religious belief and ritual. An obvious example of this point of view would be to say that the Christian festivals of Christmas and Easter are based on the myths of Christ's birth and resurrection. To call these stories 'myths' is not to say they are untrue. Religious myths are neither true nor false in the sense that statements by historians can be proved wrong by the discovery of new evidence, or scientific hypotheses can be subjected to verification or rejection by experiment. Myths are intended to state abstract truths but they always do so in the form of a story. To dismiss the story because it is demonstrably untrue or impossible is no more sensible than to tell a poet that he is claiming what is a physical impossibility when he writes (for instance):

> I saw Eternity the other night
> Like a great Ring of pure and endless light,
>   All calm as it was bright. . . .

A wiser reaction is to try to find out what he means and why intelligent people take him seriously. The same is true with myth.

Peleus and Thetis (continued)

THE JUDGEMENT OF PARIS

The Apple of Discord (as it came to be called) had the effect that was

The shepherd Paris judging the three goddesses: Athena, Hera and Aphrodite

intended. Three goddesses claimed it: Hera, the wife of Zeus and goddess of marriage; Athena, goddess of wisdom and military skill; and Aphrodite, goddess of sexual love and feminine charm. They at once ceased to behave with the graciousness of royalty condescending to honour the wedding of a commoner who has married above himself – which was the spirit in which the happy occasion had begun – but instead began to squabble like a trio of catty carnival queens at a beauty contest. Zeus, when asked to be judge, acted like any male who cannot bear to risk incurring feminine wrath, and took the cowardly course of shuffling the responsibility on to someone else. This was a poor herdsman who was leading an idyllic life on the slopes of Mount Ida in Asia Minor, blissfully sharing his cave with a charming and talented nymph, named Oenone.

It turned out that the poor shepherd – as Zeus very well knew – was no true shepherd but the long-lost son of Priam, King of Troy, by name Paris. The story of his judgement is notorious. Each goddess tried to win the apple by bribery: Hera offered a splendid kingdom; Athena, glory in war;

and Aphrodite marriage to the most beautiful woman in the world. This was not the first time in Greek mythology that the lure of a beautiful woman had been used by an immortal to overcome mortal prudence; and not the first time that male susceptibility brought catastrophe on the human race.

This time the catastrophe was the Trojan War, which came about because the most beautiful woman in the world happened to be already married to a Greek king – Menelaos; and from his palace she had to be enticed or kidnapped. Whether she went voluntarily or not is disputed, but Paris was a very handsome man, and had already won the devotion of Oenone, whom he now abandoned without a qualm, although she earnestly warned him what would happen if he married Helen. So Aphrodite got the apple and fulfilled her promise; but almost all the princes of Greece were under an obligation to help Menelaos to recapture his wife. The great expedition which undertook this task brought tragedy to nearly every royal house in Greece, and total destruction to Troy and Priam and all his family, including Paris. But Zeus was, on the whole, pleased, because the world had been getting overpopulated.

THE MARRIAGE OF PELEUS AND THETIS

The marriage was blessed with a son, Achilles, who in due course became, as prophesied, the strongest, bravest and swiftest of mortals. Soon after his birth, Thetis attempted to make him immortal. (Immortality was normally reserved for those whose mother and father were *both* divine.) There are several different accounts of how this was to be done. One story related that she had already had six sons, all of whom she had put into the fire in order to burn away the mortal parts that they had inherited from their father, and so give them immortality; after which she sent them to Olympos to live with the gods. She now wished to do this with Achilles; but when – in legend, folk-tale or myth – a mortal man marries an immortal bride, the marriage nearly always ends in misunderstanding and disaster. This marriage was true to type. Peleus had been mystified by the disappearance of his first six sons, and when he happened to see Thetis putting the new-born child into the fire, he rushed forward and plucked him out before the flames had burnt away more than the child's ankle-bone.

The consequence of this rash act was that Thetis, annoyed at his blundering interference, deserted husband, home and child, and returned to the depths of the sea to live with her father and her forty-nine sisters. Peleus, however, replaced the burnt ankle-bone with the ankle-bone of the swiftest of the giants, whose skeleton he dug up for this purpose.

Another story, better known to us, but less well known to the Greeks, relates that Thetis tried to make Achilles *invulnerable*, not immortal; and did this by dipping him in the Styx (the river that flows through the Underworld). However, she forgot to immerse the heel by which she was holding him, and the result was fatal. Victorious in innumerable fights, he was eventually killed by Paris – no great fighter, but a very skilful archer – who, with a little help from the god Apollo, shot him in the heel, just where the Achilles tendon is, with a poisoned arrow.

THE YOUTH OF ACHILLES

Achilles could have avoided his early death. The Fates had decreed that he could choose to go to Troy to die in battle, young and famous; or he could choose to stay at home and live without glory to a ripe old age.

Knowing this, Thetis arranged for him to be disguised as a girl and brought up among the daughters of Lykomedes, king of the island of Skyros. This was not a very successful stratagem, as he seduced one of the king's daughters (and had a son by her, called Neoptolemos), and when the Greek generals came to enrol him in their army, the cunning Odysseus had no difficulty in making him reveal his true sex and nature by a simple trick. He invited all the court ladies to choose from some suitably feminine presents he had brought with him, among which he placed a sword and some armour. As they were choosing their presents, a trumpet-blast was heard from outside the palace, accompanied by the sound of fighting. All this was stage-managed by Odysseus. Immediately the true females ran away with shrill cries while Achilles threw off his feminine dress, seized the sword and armour, and rushed off to find the fight.

ACHILLES AT TROY: THE INTERVENTIONS OF THETIS

When Achilles went to Troy, leading his father's subjects, the Myrmidons, he took with him the gifts his father had received from the gods at his wedding: two swift and immortal horses, children of the West Wind; and the golden arms and armour which were destined to play a fateful part in the fighting when he lent them to his beloved friend Patroklos.

Thetis was a devoted mother, and suffered for all the sorrows of her son. Three times she pleaded with the gods on Olympos on his behalf. The first occasion was when he was insulted by King Agamemnon (Lord of Mycenae and Commander-in-chief of the Greeks) in a dispute over the possession of a female captive acquired during a raid. Achilles refused to fight any more, and Thetis persuaded Zeus to make the battle go against the Greeks, so that they would miss Achilles all the more keenly. The second was after Patroklos had been killed in Achilles' armour, and Hector, the Trojan leader, had stripped it off his corpse and was wearing it himself: Thetis went to Hephaistos and begged him successfully for a new set of armour, even more wonderful than the armour he had lost. The third occasion was after Achilles' death: when she had completed the arrangements for his elaborate funeral, she successfully petitioned Poseidon for an island (the White Island) in the Black Sea; there she took his spirit, gave him Helen as a wife, and left him jousting and running races with other heroes to all eternity. (But the *Odyssey* says that Helen went back to Sparta to live in respectable middle-aged domesticity with Menelaos, while Achilles went down to the Underworld and grumbled that 'life' there was more dismal than it was for the most miserable peasant on earth.)

THE GOOD DEEDS OF THETIS

Why was it that the gods were invariably ready to do favours for Thetis? They were not always so obliging to one another. No doubt she was very beautiful and desirable, seeing that both Zeus and his brother Poseidon had wanted to marry her; but she had other qualities also. Unlike the other gods and goddesses, who were often selfish, arrogant and vindictive, Thetis was sensible and compassionate. When the gods, led by Hera, conspired against Zeus, they tied him up with a hundred knots and put his irresistible thunderbolts out of reach; but Thetis, foreseeing endless strife and confusion if civil war were to break out in heaven again, rescued him by sending the hundred-armed giant Briareos to undo all the knots at once. When Hera gave birth to Hephaistos she was disgusted by the ugliness of her son; so she picked him up and threw him out of Olympos, and he fell all the way down from heaven into the sea. Thetis rescued him, and she and her sister Eurynome hid him in an underwater cave, where he spent nine years making them bracelets and other ornaments, until his mother, learning of his skill, took him back to Olympos and set him up with a proper blacksmith's shop, where he made furniture for the other gods, and robots and self-propelling tables, and sometimes suits of armour; and, no doubt, jewellery for his mother Hera. But for the rest of eternity he limped as a result of his fall. In the same underwater cave Thetis received and comforted Dionysos when he and his followers were being persecuted by Lykurgos, king of the Thracians, in the period before the Dionysiac rites had been accepted among the Greeks.

So much for Thetis; beautiful, sweet-natured and sensible: a marvellous mother but a disappointing wife. But what of her husband Peleus? He was lonely and insecure while Achilles was fighting at Troy, but protected by the terror that Achilles inspired. After the death of Achilles he was driven out of his kingdom by his enemies; and Neoptolemos, his grandson, hastening home from the sack of Troy arrived to find that he had died in exile.

Reflections on the myth of Peleus and Thetis

First, is it true? Obviously not, in any literal or scientific sense. In any other sense, then? Perhaps; but that is a profound and complex question which no one should try to answer until he has considered the many forms that myths take, and the theories that have been put forward about their origins. There are *elements* of the Peleus-Thetis story that *might* be true even in the literal sense. Heinrich Schliemann, the self-made millionaire and Homeric scholar, was laughed at for squandering money on an expedition to dig up a mythical city; but he persisted in digging where his study of the *Iliad* told him Troy ought to be, and found not one Troy but nine – that is to say he found the remains of nine cities, all but the first built on the ruins of a predecessor; and more than one of them had evidently been sacked and burnt. Did Achilles, then, fight and die there, and was it his son Neoptolemos who led the troops which sacked and burnt it? This part of the story falls under the heading of legend, and will have to be considered in the next chapter.

MORGANS AND MERMAIDS

Did a beautiful goddess come out of the sea and marry a mortal? Have people really seen an enormous monster swimming on the surface of Loch Ness? It may one day be possible to answer the second question: the first question is meaningless. There are innumerable folk-tales about beautiful female creatures who live in the seas off Brittany or in Welsh lakes. They are called Morgans, and scholars derive this name from a Celtic river goddess, Matrona, who also gave her name to the French river Marne. Morgan le Fay, a sinister character in the Arthurian stories, was one of these. Morgans sometimes fall in love with young men (according to one version of the story Thetis fell in love with Peleus when she saw him sailing with Jason and the Argonauts in search of the Golden Fleece). The embrace of Morgans is usually fatal, though occasionally they carry off their mortal lovers to live happily at the bottom of the sea. There is a Yorkshire tale called 'Johnny and the Mermaid', in which Johnny lies in wait on the seashore, like Peleus, and captures a mermaid because he has been told they can grant 'wishes three'. She struggles, but he holds on, and at last she says, 'Quit and have'. So he lets go and gets his wishes.

Closer to the Thetis story are the tales from the Shetland Islands of seals which come ashore and shed their skins and turn into beautiful girls. If a man can steal and hide the skin, the seal-girl is obliged to remain in human form, and he may marry her and have children by her; but if she finds the skin, she is liable to put it on and desert husband, child and home, and return to the sea. Sometimes it is some unkindness or tactlessness on the part of her husband which sends her back to the sea. Variations of such stories, in which the bride is a swan, or a fish, are found from Alaska to the Pacific islands.

TRAGIC AND FRIVOLOUS

Noticeable about the Peleus story is the range and variation of the mood. The undignified behaviour of the goddesses at the beauty contest is comic and frivolous; the plight of Peleus, abandoned by his goddess wife, and deprived in old age of the support of his son and grandson, pathetic; the fate of Achilles, Troy and Priam, heroic and tragic. But it would be a mistake to assume that the frivolous part of the story is *necessarily* the least significant. If the theories of a French scholar should turn out to be correct, the Judgement of Paris is a very serious matter indeed. Paris is being offered a choice between three ways of life: sovereignty; military skill; and fertility and earthly pleasures. The welfare of society depends on valuing them in that order of preference. Paris puts the lowest first, and the message of the myth is that this brings disaster to himself and to his country.

INCONSISTENCIES OF MYTHOLOGY

Noticeable also about the Peleus-Thetis story are the implausibilities and inconsistencies. It ignores many awkward questions, such as: how do you, even if you are as brave and determined as Peleus, hang on to someone who has turned herself into fire or water? Why, if Achilles was so valiant, did he allow himself to be hidden among a group of girls? Why, if Zeus was omnipotent, and had decided that Thetis must marry a mortal, and had gone to the trouble of finding the best bridegroom available, did Thetis make things so difficult for Peleus? Why could not she explain to Peleus that she was putting Achilles into the fire to make him immortal? And so on. There are two reasons that can be given for such inconsistencies.

Independent sources

First, the Greek myths, as we know them, have been woven by poets and mythographers out of many quite independent stories into one intricate, superficially coherent, system of mythology in which the stories dovetail into one another. These stories come from many different sources, were told differently in different parts of Greece, and in many cases originally had nothing to do with the hero to whom they eventually became attached (just as the cat story became attached to Sir Richard Whittington). Furthermore, the gods and heroes of the stories were often composite personalities – they had acquired characteristics, and sometimes extra names, from gods and heroes belonging to other peoples. Thus Phoebos Apollo, also called Smintheus or Lykeios, was the god of archery *and* healing, *and* prophecy, and eventually of the sun too; and Artemis, also called Phoebe, was the goddess of virginity and hunting, yet in Ephesos (where St Paul got into trouble with her image-makers), she was worshipped as a giver of fertility. She was also the protectress of women in childbirth, and identified with the moon. For all these reasons the myths were full of ambiguities and inconsistencies and loose ends which could never be completely tidied up, however hard a patient mythographer might try. But it suited the poets, because they had a free choice from many variations of any story they were interested in. We have seen that there were two versions of what happened to Achilles after his death. Similarly, there were two quite different versions of how he was killed; and for the ending of the Peleus-Thetis marriage there were at least three versions – the one told above, another which related that Thetis left Peleus only when he was getting old and crotchety, and then because it is not permitted for a goddess to be associated with decay and death; and a third version, that of the dramatist Euripides, in which Thetis tells the aged Peleus to wait in the cave where he first captured her, and she will come and carry him off to live with her for ever at the bottom of the sea.

The logic of story-telling

The second reason is that story-telling has its own logic, quite different from the logic of philosophers and not concerned with consistency or realism. What this logic is, is yet another matter under dispute; but it is quite clear that those who tell and listen to myths are not bothered by implausibility and contradictions. Both the Old and New Testaments contain many contradictions and ambiguities, but for centuries they worried no one but theologians and a few priests. The Greeks had no theologians and, practically speaking, no professional priests; and only a few pedantic antiquarians worried about difficulties such as the age of Helen of Troy, or of Penelope.

THE WRECK OF XERXES' ARMADA

One final question. Did the Greeks believe their own myths?

When Xerxes, Great King of Persia, was leading his immense army and equally immense fleet into Greece, he suffered a serious disaster to the fleet. It had anchored off the coast between a city called Casthanea and

Cape Sepias (*sepias* is the Greek for cuttlefish), but a sudden storm blew up and scattered those of his ships whose crews had not been able to beach them. Herodotus, the historian, writing about fifty years later, describes the storm thus:

> It was quite irresistible, and at the lowest count the Persians lost four hundred ships, innumerable men and a vast amount of treasure. . . . It lasted three days. On the fourth day, the Persian priests calmed it by making sacrifices to Thetis and the Nereids. Or possibly it decided to subside of its own accord. The reason why they sacrificed to Thetis was that they heard from the Ionian Greeks that it was from this spot that she was carried off by Peleus, and that all the coast of Cape Sepias was sacred to her, and to the other daughters of Nereus. [Herodotus VII, chap. 191]

Herodotus was born and grew up in a Greek city on the coast of Asia Minor, and he spent part of his life at Athens. In Asia Minor the speculations of the first scientists had been going on for over a century; Athens was in his time the intellectual centre of Greece. Nevertheless, though he does not commit himself to saying that Thetis calmed the storm, he does not treat the Persian sacrifices as superstitious nonsense: but rather as a modern historian might relate that a Thanksgiving Service was held in St Paul's Cathedral in 1940 for victory in the Battle of Britain.

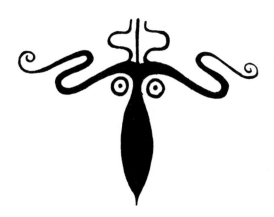

2

Legends I

Legendary heroes

ARTHUR

W A S there ever a King Arthur, and did he have a Round Table, and knights who went in search of the Holy Grail? There is no evidence for his existence, let alone for his exploits, that would impress a sceptical historian; but he was taken very seriously by King Henry II of England, by Queen Elizabeth I; and now by the learned members of the Camelot Research Committee who are excavating, among other sites, Cadbury Hill in Somerset, in the hope that it can be shown to be Arthur's Camelot. And if you go to Hadrian's Wall, near Milecastle 34 you can see the site of Sewingshields Castle, beneath which, according to a story once widely known in Northern England, there is a vault where a farmer once discovered Arthur, his Queen Guinivere, his lords, ladies and faithful hounds, sitting entranced until someone shall blow a horn which lies on a table beside the entrance. Then he is destined to awake and lead his knights to victory against the enemies of the British People. (Arthur is presumably still there, as the farmer was too dim-witted, or too sensible, to blow the horn; and no one else has been able to discover the entrance to the vault.)

ETZEL, GUNTER AND KRIMHILD

If Arthur existed, then his period was about AD 500, shortly after the Roman legions had left Britain for good. The Romans left because their continental empire was collapsing under the blows struck by one invasion of barbarian tribes after another. The most terrible of these were the hordes of savage horsemen led by Attila the Hun, who caused such terror and destruction wherever he went that he boasted that the grass never grew on the spot where his horse had trod. In the prime of life, when he was pausing between one campaign of devastation and another, he suddenly died. On the previous night he had celebrated, in his encampment near the Danube, his wedding to the latest of his many wives, a beautiful

Burgundian girl named Ildico. In the morning he was found dead of a haemorrhage. During his reign, one of his armies had annihilated a Burgundian force under their king Gundaharius, killing Gundaharius and all his family. These facts are known with fair certainty from Latin chronicles of more or less contemporary date (though the nationality of Ildico can only be guessed at). Four, five and six centuries later, legends were being told in which Etzel (Attli, in the Scandinavian versions), having married the sister of the Niflung chieftains, treacherously invites them to his palace to extort from them the secret of their fabulous treasure. Their sister tries to warn them, but in vain: they are all murdered for refusing to disclose its hiding-place. Their sister then avenges them by murdering Etzel and his sons, and burns the palace over them. About AD 1200 this story was combined – not for the first time – with stories about the invincible warrior Siegfried. Siegfried, so the stories told, had made himself invulnerable (except for one spot between his shoulder-blades) by bathing in the blood of the dragon which guarded the treasure of the Nibelungs. He had killed the dragon and got the treasure. In the combined story (the *Nibelungenlied*, the 'Song of the Nibelungs') he woos the athletic Queen Brunhild of Iceland on behalf of Gunther (Gundaharius) in exchange for his own marriage to Gunther's sister, Krimhild (Ildico?). A fierce and bitter rivalry springs up between the two queens, which leads to the murder of Siegfried, treacherously stabbed (in his vulnerable spot) with the connivance of Gunther; and this, in turn, leads to the massacre of Gunther and his brothers and comrades-in-arms in the palace of Etzel (now Krimhild's second husband) where Krimhild had lured them to avenge the murder of Siegfried.

CHARLEMAGNE AND ROLAND

About three hundred years after the time of Arthur, and three hundred and twenty-five years precisely after the death of Attila, Charlemagne, Emperor of the Franks, went campaigning in Spain. He had been invited to support certain Mohammedan nobles against the Saracen (Mohammedan) Emir of Cordova. On his return to France, his rearguard was ambushed and annihilated by some Basque (Christian) mountaineers. This much we know from the *Life of Charlemagne*, written by his chaplain Einhart. Einhart adds that in the battle there died: 'Eggihardt, the Chamberlain; Anselm, the Count of the Palace; and Hruodlandus, the Count of Brittany'. This piece of history is confirmed from Saracen sources, written in Arabic. Not very long after the Norman conquest of England, and about the time of the early crusades, there was written in Norman French the *Song of Roland*. Roland (Hruodlandus) is now Charlemagne's nephew and leading warrior, and for Charlemagne he has conquered Acquitaine, Apulia, Bavaria,

Constantinople, England and Scotland. But he has an enemy, his step-father Ganelon, who plots treacherously with the Saracens to fake a pretence of making peace so as to trap Roland with the rearguard of the army as Charlemagne marches back across the Pyrenees to France. The plot is successful, and Roland dies after fighting against tremendous odds. With his dying breath he blows his horn, and summons Charlemagne to avenge him. Charlemagne returns with the main army, and fights a battle with Baligant, the Emir of Babylon, whom the Saracens have summoned to their aid. The battle ends in a single combat between Charlemagne, who is two hundred years old, and the Babylonian Emir, who has outlived Virgil and even Homer (but both Charlemagne and Baligant are, despite their age, the finest fighters – Roland apart – in their respective armies). Charlemagne is victorious and Christianity triumphant over Mohammedanism; all the dead Christians go to Paradise, all the dead Mohammedans to Hell. The Spanish Emir's wife, Bramimond, is brought to Aix-la-Chapelle (Charlemagne's historical capital) and baptized: and Ganelon, after trial by Ordeal of Battle, is condemned to be torn apart by four stallions.

The historical background of Greek legend

CRETE

At Knossos in Crete there was already a very small town four thousand years before the birth of Christ. This was in the Stone Age. With the Bronze Age, in the third millennium BC, new waves of immigrants settled beside the inhabitants of this town and intermarried with them and carried their civilisation to a higher degree of refinement. Between 2000 and 1400 BC it was a very impressive civilisation indeed, and unique in its time for its peaceful and pleasure-loving character. The Cretans built enormous and elaborate palaces, and elegant private houses containing bathrooms, lavatories, halls and interior staircases. They adorned these with pictures of men and women dressed in a style which would be considered fashionable and sophisticated today. Other wall-paintings showed men and girls somersaulting over the backs of long-horned bulls, boxers wearing gloves, and girls dancing; or flowers, fish, trees and animals. In their shrines they placed as religious emblems three-legged altars, bulls' horns and double axes; and they made clay or ivory statuettes of their goddess – or goddesses – dressed like their own womenfolk and holding snakes or birds or animals. They knew the art of writing and they traded with the other islands of the Eastern Mediterranean and beyond. It is possible – but there is no direct evidence – that the ruler of Knossos was styled Minos (that is to say, it was a title, not a proper name) and was treated as a divine being,

as were the contemporary Pharaohs of Egypt. In about 1450 BC part of
Crete was devastated, possibly when the volcano on the island of Thera
blew up. For the next half-century or so Knossos was more prosperous
than ever, but a new form of writing was adopted for recording lists of
palace property in the Greek language. (This is the so-called Linear B
script: the previous script, termed Linear A, was used for writing in some
other language than Greek and has never been deciphered.) There are also
other archaeological indications that at some period after 1600 BC control
of the island had passed to Greek-speaking rulers. Somewhere around
1400 BC Knossos and all the other main cities of Crete were destroyed and
never rebuilt.

A Cretan brooch

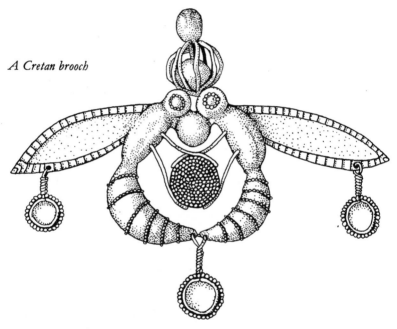

MYCENAEAN GREECE

'Minoan' Crete is so called by modern scholars because of the legendary
King Minos of Knossos, who was supposed to have ruled all Crete.
'Mycenaean' Greece is so called because at Mycenae the first and most
extensive remains were unearthed of a civilisation whose language was
Greek, and which was nearly as rich and impressive as that of Crete. Many
other sites have since been found on the mainland of Greece and on the
islands, and of these half-a-dozen or so were once powerful cities, famous
in legend. Whether the development of these cities was due to the immi-
gration of a new warrior people or to some political upheaval in Greece is
unknown; but a new type of society had arisen, which expended consider-

able wealth (whether acquired by trade or plunder or both, no one can tell) on building immense beehive-shaped tombs in the hillsides for its kings as well as simpler graves for lesser chieftains. These they buried with quantities of beautiful and precious armour, ornaments and banqueting vessels.[1] Remains from the tombs show that they used chariots for fighting, and as the chariot is an expensive item of military equipment, and requires skill and training to handle, this might have helped to bring about a social revolution to favour the successful few against the many. The evidence from Crete makes it clear that some of these Greek-speaking warriors succeeded in making themselves masters of Knossos, and so controlling the island, but it does not show where they came from.

Soon after Knossos had been overthrown, the mainland Mycenaeans turned some of their energies from building tombs to building huge fortified palaces (the palaces of Crete were never fortified) at Mycenae, Tiryns, Thebes, Athens and a number of other places (though, strangely, the large palace at Pylos was not fortified). In and around these palaces were employed large numbers of female slaves to weave cloth from wool, and a considerable number of scribes to keep detailed – not to say pernickety – accounts of the women's labours, and of the palace property, and of the sheep and oxen which were the King's property or, possibly, due to him as tribute.

THE DARK AGE OF GREECE

Not long after 1200 BC (which is roughly the date at which the seventh city of Troy was overthrown), all these palaces (except that at Athens) were destroyed and abandoned. The art of writing was forgotten, and the arts of pottery and metalwork declined drastically. An age of confusion and barbarity had overtaken Greece, and the remains of the Minoan and Mycenaean civilizations – their palaces, their paintings, their armour, jewellery and their documents – were gradually buried beneath the earth, and their memory lived on only in the songs of minstrels.

EXCAVATION AND RECONSTRUCTION

In the last hundred years some of the palaces have been unearthed, and some of the documents pieced together and deciphered by the joint labours of excavators and philologists. The surviving documents have so far turned out to be rather dull lists of slaves and sheep and offerings to the various gods, together with a few uninformative military instructions; and they survived solely because they were written on soft clay which was accidentally baked hard when the palaces were sacked and burnt.

---

[1] No doubt the objects buried with the kings were even more splendid, but their tombs were all looted long ago.

Scholars have also assembled and interpreted tablets from the rediscovered capital of the Hittite Empire, which fell at about the same time as Troy VII. These are much more informative than the Greek tablets, and record diplomatic correspondence which gives some hints as to what was going on in the Eastern Mediterranean at the time.

However, the excavators and philologists can reconstruct the lost world of the Minoans and Mycenaeans only in outline: they cannot recreate for us the personality of a single king, queen, warrior or scribe, nor even the gods or goddesses they worshipped.

LEGEND AND REALITY

By contrast the traditions that were transmitted through the songs of the minstrels were full of vivid incident and striking personalities. How much each generation of minstrels distorted, exaggerated and embroidered on the events they were telling, and added to them incidents from quite different sources, is an open question; but we have seen what happened to Charlemagne's expedition to Spain, and to the death of Attila and the destruction of a Burgundian war-band.

To those who believe that Homer's *Iliad* is – gods and goddesses apart – basically a true account of a real siege, we can put the question, 'What should we believe about Charlemagne and Roland and the Saracens, or about Attila and the Burgundians, if they were separated from us by three or four centuries of unbroken barbarism and illiteracy, through which no documents had survived except for palace inventories for one single year?'

On the other hand, those who believe in the historical reality of the *Iliad* can retort that, when Schliemann dug up the mound of Hissarlik, he *did* find the nine cities of Troy, and when he dug up a hill-top overlooking the Plain of Argos, he *did* find a palace built of massive masonry, and huge graves in which were still lying splendid weapons of gold and ivory, and death masks of gold and electrum. He had not gazed upon the face of Agamemnon, as he over-optimistically cabled the King of Greece in 1876, but he had uncovered the palace of a wealthy and powerful king, who might well have led an expedition against Troy, or any other city in the Eastern Mediterranean.

The cities of legend

Many cities are named in Homer's list of the contingents who fought at Troy, but the legends themselves are largely concentrated on a handful of famous places: Troy, Thebes, Athens, and the cities of the Argive Plain –

Mycenae, Tiryns and Argos. Excavation has revealed that all these cities – whether they remained important like Thebes, Athens and Argos; or shrank into insignificance, like Troy, Mycenae and Tiryns – were, in Mycenaean times, powerful fortresses. Their walls were built of blocks of stone so massive that the later Greeks said they must have been built by the giant Cyclopes: for in classical Greece it was hard to imagine the kind of society which could organise the quarrying, transportation and placing of such immense sections of masonry.

The legends that belonged, or became attached, to these Mycenaean cities were woven together until it became possible to provide a continuous 'history' for them, while still allowing for the co-existence of rival versions which could only be denied, never disproved.

The foundation

The kingdom of Troy was founded, shortly after the Flood (see p. 73), by Dardanos, who built Dardania on the slopes of Mount Ida. And who was Dardanos? All good heroic pedigrees began with a god, and the royal family of Troy was no exception. Dardanos was the son of Zeus by one of those daughters of Atlas who now shine in the night sky under the name of Pleiades.

He was succeeded by his son Erichthonios, who was the richest of men and owned three thousand mares, so beautiful that the North Wind fell in love with them, and begot on them some steeds so swift that their feet never touched the ground. Erichthonios' son was Tros, who gave his name to the district known as the Troad, and to the city itself, and had three sons. These were Ilos, Assarakos and Ganymedes. The youngest of these, Ganymedes, was so extraordinarily handsome that the gods wanted him as their cup-bearer. Therefore Zeus turned himself into an eagle and whisked him up to Heaven, where he happily attends all the banquets of the gods, and pours red nectar out of a golden bowl. In compensation Zeus gave Tros two horses, superbly swift and handsome, and immortal. Assarakos, the middle son, has only one claim to distinction: he was grandfather to Anchises, and so great-grandfather to Aeneas, who, if we are to believe Virgil, founded the Roman race, and was the ancestor of Julius Caesar and Augustus. The eldest son, Ilos, inherited the kingdom and resited, or rebuilt, the city, which was called Ilion after him, as well as Troy after his father.

The perfidy of Laomedon

Ilos' son and successor was Laomedon. It was during Laomedon's reign that there occurred in Heaven that revolt of the gods which nearly overthrew the power of Zeus. After he had been rescued through the intervention of Thetis (see p. 18), Zeus punished the chief conspirators, Poseidon and Apollo, by condemning them to work for a whole year helping Laomedon to build the walls of Troy, which had hitherto remained unwalled. They summoned from Greece a mortal, Aiakos, son of Zeus and father of Peleus, to help them; and, not surprisingly, Aiakos' part of the walls was the weakest. (But Homer says that only Poseidon worked on the walls, Apollo merely looked after Laomedon's cattle.)

Although they were gods and acting on Zeus' orders, nonetheless Poseidon and Apollo expected just payment for their labours. Laomedon defrauded them of this, and was made to suffer for it. An appalling monster came out of the sea and caused death and destruction over the whole Troad. The only remedy – so Laomedon was told by the oracle of Zeus – was to chain his daughter Hesione naked to a rock for the monster to eat.

Fortunately for Hesione, Herakles happened to pass by as she was waiting to be devoured. He was returning from his Ninth Labour, the capture of the belt of Hippolyte, the Amazon Queen. He broke Hesione's chains and went to Laomedon, offering to kill the monster. In return he asked for the two horses which had been given to Tros in recompense for the kidnapping of Ganymedes. Laomedon agreed to the bargain; but he seems to have been unable to learn from his mistakes, because he again broke a promise. Herakles killed the monster, but when he claimed the reward Laomedon substituted mortal horses for the two that had come into the royal stables as a present from Zeus. Herakles was never a character to be trifled with. He collected an expeditionary force, sacked Troy, and killed Laomedon and all his sons except the infant Priam, who thereupon succeeded to the throne.

The reign of Priam

During Priam's reign the fame and prosperity of Troy grew greater than ever. He had fifty sons and many daughters. The most notable of these children were Hector, the twins Helenos and Kassandra, and Paris. Hector and Paris are too well known to need description. Of Helenos and Kassandra it is sufficient to say that they both received the gift of prophecy. For Kassandra this was a back-handed gift which had come to her from the god Apollo. He fell in love with her, she promised to sleep with him in return for the gift, then – like her grandfather Laomedon – she went back on her promise. So Apollo let her keep the gift (a god's gift cannot be recalled), but ensured that no one would ever believe her. Nor was Helenos' gift of prophecy able to avert the doom of Troy. When Paris had been born, his mother Hecuba had dreamed that she had been delivered of a flaming torch. This was rightly interpreted to mean that her child would bring destruction on his city; so Hecuba was told to kill him.

However, she made the mistake of merely having him exposed to die on Mount Ida. He was adopted by a she-bear, and survived to grow up into a handsome shepherd and become the lover of the nymph Oenone, with whom he used to go hunting on Mount Ida. And that is where the three goddesses found him when he was chosen to judge which of them was the most beautiful.

The Siege of Troy

As we have seen in Chapter 1, the warnings of Oenone to Paris, of what would happen if he eloped with Helen, went unheeded and she was duly proved right. A mighty expedition to recover Helen was led by Agamemnon, King of Mycenae and brother of Menelaos, and for nine years fighting raged round the city walls. The climax of the siege came in the tenth year. Achilles killed Hector and was in turn killed by Paris. Paris himself did not survive long. He was mortally wounded by Philoctetes who had inherited the miraculous bow of Herakles and his poisoned arrows. Paris could have been healed by Oenone (she knew the arts of healing as well as those of prophecy), but she was still angry with him for his desertion of her, and she refused. She later relented, but it was too late and she hanged herself in remorse.

Even now the Trojans refused to give up Helen. Two of Paris' brothers quarrelled over her: Helenos and Deiphobos. Priam awarded her to Deiphobos, so Helenos left Troy in anger. Shortly afterwards he was captured by the Greeks and readily betrayed to them his prophetic knowledge that Troy could be captured only if the assault were led by Achilles' son, Neoptolemos. So Neoptolemos was fetched from the court of Lykomedes at Skyros (see p. 17).

The Sack of Troy and its Aftermath

All that was now required was the stratagem of the Wooden Horse. Seeing the Greek fleet apparently sailing back to Greece, the Trojans gave themselves up to feasting and celebration. While they were sleeping off the effects of this, the Wooden Horse disgorged its inmates. The sentries were quickly cut down and the gates thrown open, and the Greek forces, who had crept back under cover of darkness, burst in. Made vicious by ten years of frustration, they slaughtered, burnt and pillaged all through the night. Priam was butchered on the altar of Zeus. Deiphobos was betrayed by Helen, anxious to regain the favour of the Greeks, and killed by Odysseus. Kassandra was raped by Ajax, the son of Oileus, on the altar of Athena; and Hector's infant son hurled from the battlements. All the men were slaughtered and all the women carried off to slavery, except for one daughter of Priam who was sacrificed at the tomb of Achilles.

The only son of Priam's to survive was Helenos, who settled in what is now Albania and founded a kingdom there. His twin sister, Kassandra, was less fortunate. After her rape by Ajax, she was apportioned to Agamemnon in his share of the spoil. She became his concubine, and was murdered with him by his wife Klytaimnestra. She foretold both murders but, as always, no one would believe her.

The Homecoming of the Greeks

The Greeks had little joy of their victory. Many of them were drowned in a terrible storm on the way home. Others, such as Agamemnon and Odysseus, returned to kingdoms which had become disloyal in their absence. Three generations after the sack of Troy all the cities which had sent heroes to Troy were destroyed and their royal families killed, or in flight. The descendants of Herakles had returned to claim their inheritance.

And Helen, the cause of all the trouble? Menelaos raged through the palace of Priam, intent on wreaking vengeance upon his faithless wife. At last he confronted her in her bedroom. She pointed to the lifeless corpse of Deiphobos, and slipping off her robes, stood naked before her husband. Her beauty was so great that he threw away his sword and forgave her, and took her back to live all the rest of their lives in domestic respectability in Sparta.

As has been hinted already (p. 21), a few literal-minded Greeks in classical times were worried by the problem of Helen's age. They had worked out by impeccable mythological reckoning that she must have been fifty when carried off by Paris, and therefore sixty when she recaptivated Menelaos by her beauty. But, with these few exceptions, the Greeks gave as little thought to such problems as most Christians have given to the problem of the geographical location of the Garden of Eden.

COMMENT

So perished Troy, 'windy Ilion', the city of the horse-rearing Trojans. To those who wish to extract as much history from legend as it can be made to yield, we can concede that the plain of Troy is windy, and that a remarkable number of bones of horses were dug up in the excavations, though not enough to reconstruct the three thousand mares of Erichthonios. It must also be admitted that, according to Homer, Andromache was always begging Hector to stop risking his life in open warfare and instead to concentrate his forces in defence of the one weak spot in the defences, presumably where the walls had been built by the mortal Aiakos; and that Dörpfeld, who continued Schliemann's excavations, claimed to have discovered that the weakest place in the walls of Troy VII was just where (according to his reckoning) Andromache had wanted Hector to make his stand.

The slaying of Priam by Neoptolemos

Note

According to the best-known legend Neoptolemos killed Priam on the altar of Zeus. Some said that for this sacrilege he was prevented by Apollo from ever returning home. Homer says he *did* return home, laden with booty, and there married Hermione, daughter of Menelaos and Helen. All, however, were agreed that he died violently at Delphi, killed either in a riot stirred up by Orestes (who wanted his cousin Hermione for himself), or by Apollo, or by Orestes personally. Later generations tended to see Neoptolemos as a savage and efficient killer, lacking the glamour and chivalry of his father: perhaps this is the sort of debunking that great warriors often undergo when the glamour of war itself has begun to look tarnished.

The royal house of Troy was brought to destruction by the intermingling of its destiny with that of the royal house of the Tantalids.

Tantalos

Tantalos was a prince of Asia Minor who was so wicked that a special torment was arranged for him in Hades for all eternity. He stands in a pool of water, but every time he bends down to drink, the water flows away and leaves only parched earth. Above him are spread the branches of fruit-trees from which dangle luscious fruits – pears, apples, figs, pomegranates and olives – but every time he reaches up for them, a puff of wind blows them away. This is what it means to *tantalise*. When one comes to enquire what wickedness it was that deserved such a merciless punishment, one finds that the circumstances and nature of his deeds were bizarre. First, being invited to attend the banquets of the gods – an extraordinary privilege granted to no other mortal – he stole some of the nectar and ambrosia (which confer immortality on those who partake of them) and gave it to his mortal friends. Then, entertaining the gods in his turn, he served them up his own son Pelops in a stew. Being gods they immediately recognised the food and rejected it with repulsion, except for Demeter, whose mind was not on what she was doing as she had lately lost her daughter Persephone. She ate the shoulder. Tantalos was punished as has been described, and the gods reconstituted Pelops, giving him an ivory shoulder to replace that part which had been eaten by Demeter.

Pelops

Pelops left Asia Minor and went to Southern Greece where he entered the contest for the hand of Hippodameia, the daughter of the King of Elis, then the most important kingdom in Southern Greece. The contest was a chariot race from Elis to the altar of Poseidon at the Isthmus of Corinth: the prize of victory was the beautiful Hippodameia in marriage, and succession to the kingdom: the price of defeat was to be transfixed by the spear of Oenomaos, her father, as he overtook you. Pelops was the thirteenth suitor to enter the contest. The heads of the previous twelve were nailed for him to see over the door of Oenomaos' house. The truth was that Oenomaos was in love with his own daughter, and was determined that no one should marry her. He was confident of victory because his horses had been given to him by his father, the god Ares. Hippodameia's role in the contest was to ride in the chariot beside her doomed suitor. However, on this occasion she happened to fall in love with Pelops; and for his sake she bribed her father's charioteer, Myrtilos,

Pelops driving Hippodameia in his chariot

to tamper with his chariot. This Myrtilos did, in such a way that the wheels flew off when it was travelling at high speed and Oenomaos was dragged to his death in the wreckage. So Pelops got his bride and the kingdom; but when Myrtilos claimed as his promised reward the privilege of sleeping for one night with the beautiful Hippodameia, Pelops threw him into the sea. As he sank beneath the waves he cursed Pelops and his descendants for ever.

The curse on the Tantalids

Chrysippos

The curse wreaked havoc over four generations. Pelops had several sons by Hippodameia, and one illegitimate son, Chrysippos, who was remarkably handsome and of whom he was particularly fond. Chrysippos attracted the love of Laios, the young king of Thebes, who had been driven out by a usurper and welcomed in Elis by Pelops. In return for Pelops' hospitality Laios taught Chrysippos the art of charioteering, and when he was restored to Thebes he carried off Chrysippos with him, to the wrath and indignation of Pelops. Hippodameia was convinced that Pelops intended to leave the kingdom of Elis to Chrysippos in preference to her own sons; so she went to Thebes and murdered him there, hoping to throw suspicion for the deed on Laios. In this she was unsuccessful, and had to escape to Argos, where she killed herself.

Atreus and Thyestes

Two of Pelops' sons, Atreus and Thyestes, were thought to have been implicated in this murder and fled also. They went to Mycenae, the kingdom of the son of their sister Nikippe. This nephew of theirs was no other than Eurystheus, the tyrant who had imposed the twelve labours on Herakles.

When they arrived, Eurystheus was about to march against the children of Herakles, whom he was persecuting just as he had persecuted their father. Eurystheus was killed in the ensuing engagement, and the throne of Mycenae was offered to the two brothers. They quarrelled over which should rule. Thyestes won the first round by a piece of trickery in which he was helped by Atreus' wife, whom he had seduced: however, with the help of Zeus, Atreus outmanœuvred him in the end. Atreus then thought up a beastly plan for revenging himself for the seduction of his wife. This started a horrific game of revenge and counter-revenge, which ended with the murder of Atreus by Thyestes' son Aigisthos, and the banishment of Atreus' sons, Agamemnon and Menelaos, by Thyestes, who now took over the throne again.

Agamemnon and Menelaos

Agamemnon and Menelaos fled to the court of Tyndareos, King of Sparta. Tyndareos' wife Leda had four children whose conception and birth had been unusual. Zeus had been much impressed by her beauty when he saw her bathing in the river Eurotas, and he contrived to make love to her in the shape of a swan. She was already pregnant when this happened, and of the four children born (from two eggs) two, Helen and Polydeukes, were the children of Zeus and therefore *immortal*, and two, Klytaimnestra and Kastor, the children of Tyndareos and therefore *mortal*. Agamemnon, the elder brother, married Klytaimnestra, and with the help of his father-in-law drove Thyestes and Aigisthos out of Mycenae, and established himself there as the richest and most powerful king in the Peloponnese (as Southern Greece had come to be called in honour of his grandfather, Pelops). Menelaos married the other daughter, Helen, and succeeded Tyndareos on the throne of Sparta. What became of this marriage we have already seen. Klytaimnestra bore Agamemnon three children: a daughter, Iphigeneia, whom Agamemnon sacrificed in order to secure favourable winds for the Greek expedition to Troy when it lay storm-bound at Aulis; another daughter, Elektra; and one son, Orestes.

The murder of Agamemnon and the vengeance of Orestes

During Agamemnon's absence at Troy, Klytaimnestra, embittered by the sacrifice of her eldest child, allowed herself to be seduced by her husband's cousin, Aigisthos, who secretly returned from banishment. When Agamemnon came home in triumph, she treacherously murdered him and had Aigisthos proclaimed king in his place.

On the night of the murder Orestes was hurried out of the palace to safety by his devoted tutor. He was brought up at the court of Agamemnon's friend, King Strophios of Krisa; and there he became the lifelong friend of the king's son Pylades. Seven years after his escape from the palace he returned to avenge his father. He was welcomed by his sister, Elektra, who was devoted to the memory of their father, and whose bitter hatred of her mother was equalled only by her contempt for the usurper, Aigisthos.

With help from her and from Pylades, Orestes killed Aigisthos first, and then his own mother. For killing his mother he was driven mad by the Furies, and wandered over many lands, accompanied by the faithful Pylades, but eventually returned to Mycenae and killed Aletes, the son of Aigisthos, who had seized the throne.

He then married his cousin, Hermione, the daughter of Helen and Menelaos. They had a son, Tisamenos, in whose reign the descendants of Herakles returned to the Peloponnese and swept away the power of all the Mycenaean dynasties, and burnt their palaces (see p. 32).

COMMENT

To history we shall have to concede the importance of charioteering in Mycenaean society; and just possibly the Asiatic origins of the house of Tantalos, though there is no confirmation yet of the conjecture that Mycenaean civilisation was created by intruders from Asia Minor. And once again the story of the destructive return of the descendants of Herakles neatly harmonises with the actual collapse of Mycenaean civilisation.

Theseus abandoning Ariadne on the island of Naxos

Note

The abandonment of Ariadne by Theseus was hard to excuse. Some artists, however, portrayed him as leaving her reluctantly, at the command of Athena – a sacrifice of love to duty. There is no such suggestion made in this picture which is based on wall-paintings from Pompeii and Herculaneum.

3
Legends II

Theseus and Athens

EARLY ADVENTURES OF THESEUS

THESEUS was the son of Aithra, who was the daughter of Pittheus, King
of Troezen and brother of Atreus and Thyestes. Theseus' father was
Aigeus, King of Athens; or, alternatively, Poseidon; or both – since most
things are possible to a god, and myths abound in ambiguities.

How Theseus found the sword buried by his father beneath a stone, and
how he made his way along the coast road to join his father at Athens,
killing five bandits and a destructive sow on his way, is perhaps too well
known to need retelling. Likewise the story of his adventures in Crete,
where Ariadne, the daughter of King Minos, fell in love with him and
helped him to kill the Minotaur. And everyone knows that after one night
he abandoned Ariadne on the island of Naxos, where she was found and
taken up to Heaven by the god Dionysos.

KING THESEUS

Returning to Athens, Theseus forgot to change the black sail of his ship
for a white one, as he had promised his father he would if he were successful. So his father killed himself from grief before the ship reached port.
Becoming king in his father's place, Theseus carried out the centralisation
of the government of Attica. Previously each local centre had conducted
its own affairs, and the people of Attica had acted in unity only in time of
war. Now Theseus transferred all the administration to Athens, and so
laid the foundations for its future greatness. He then turned himself into
a constitutional monarch, leaving power to the citizen assemblies and
acting merely as commander-in-chief of the army. In this capacity he led
the Athenian forces against the Theban king Kreon, who was refusing
burial to the corpses of the Argive chieftains who had fallen in their
attempt to capture that city. He was successful in this errand of mercy,
which was only one of several acts in which he exhibited the noble
character of a leader of men always ready to come to the help of the weak
and oppressed.

In some respects, then, Theseus appears as a paragon of virtue; nevertheless his personal life continued to be irregular, not to say disreputable. He engaged in a campaign against the Amazons, and returned with their Queen Hippolyte as his bride. By her he had a son Hippolytos. He next married Phaidra, the younger sister of Ariadne (accounts differ as to what happened to Hippolyte). Phaidra fell madly in love with her stepson Hippolytos, who was addicted to hunting, and not interested in women. When he rejected her with horror, she told Theseus that he had attempted to rape her, and then killed herself. Theseus called down on the innocent Hippolytos the curse granted to him by his father Poseidon. Poseidon appeared out of the sea in the form of a bull just as Hippolytos was driving away into exile in his chariot. The horses stampeded and Hippolytos, despite his great skill as a charioteer, was dragged to his death.

THESEUS THE PHILANDERER

Apart from his three wives, Theseus had affairs with girls named Anaxo, Periboia, Iope, Aigle, Perigune and Alope: these last two were the daughters of two of the bandits he slew on the road from Troezen to Athens. Worse was to come. Theseus had become the firm friend of Perithoos, king of the Lapiths. He was at the wedding of Perithoos to Hippodameia (another Hippodameia, not the charioteering daughter of Oinomaos), at which the Centaurs got drunk and carried off the bride as well as any other women they could lay their hands on. Theseus and Perithoos then decided that they would each like to marry a daughter of Zeus, and agreed to help each other to achieve this. First, on Theseus' behalf, they went to Sparta to carry off Helen, who was then a girl of no more than twelve (some say ten) years. When they had seized her, they took her back to Attica and left her in the care of Theseus' mother Aithra until she should be old enough to marry.

Then, on Perithoos' behalf, the two friends went down to the Underworld to carry off Persephone herself. This was going too far. They reached the palace of Hades, but having incautiously accepted an invitation from their host to be seated they found themselves fixed immovably to two stone thrones which grew into their flesh. And there they had to stay, Perithoos for ever, Theseus until Herakles, who was his cousin and friend, came and rescued him, pulling him off with such violence that he left part of his buttocks behind.

THE DEATH OF THESEUS

In the meantime Helen's brothers, Kastor and Polydeukes, had led an expedition to Attica to rescue her. This they did, after ravaging Attica;

and took her back to Sparta together with Aithra, Theseus' mother, as her slave. Aithra was eventually rescued after the sack of Troy, whither she had gone with Helen when Helen eloped with Paris.

When Theseus got back from the Underworld, he found the Athenians much disillusioned with him; so he shook the dust of Athens off his feet and went to Skyros, to King Lykomedes. There he fell – or was pushed – over a cliff, and died and was buried.

Many centuries later the Athenian general and statesman, Kimon, led an expedition to Skyros and recovered the bones, which he brought back and reburied in a shrine specially built for them in the centre of Athens.

THE CHARACTER OF THESEUS

The exploits and character of Theseus are odd and suspicious. At one moment he is behaving like a statesmanlike and constitutional monarch, an example to the world of Athenian democracy, eight hundred years in advance of his time; at another he seems to be showing that anything Herakles can do, he can do almost as well, including the seduction and abandonment of nymphs and princesses. His expedition to secure burial for the dead who fell in the Theban war, and a war fought in the Peloponnese on behalf of the children of Herakles, add to his credit as a democratic champion of the victims of tyranny. But his expedition to Sparta to abduct the twelve-year-old Helen hardly becomes a middle-aged, thrice-married statesman: and the abortive attempt to kidnap Persephone is both scandalous and ridiculous.

Perhaps oddest of all is the combination of exploits connected with Crete and political activities related to the democratic movement at Athens. To a classical Greek Cretan civilisation belonged to the dim and distant past, whereas Athenian democracy was the most recent and advanced political development in the Greek world.

Theseus and Charlemagne: a comparison

CHARLEMAGNE

We know that Charlemagne lost his rearguard when returning from an unsuccessful campaign in which he had been fighting in alliance with some Saracens against other Saracens, and that the rearguard was destroyed by *Christian* Basques: whereas in the *Song of Roland* (composed in the eleventh century) he is engaged in a holy war against the wicked infidels. Significantly, in the eleventh century all Europe was being aroused by the

Pope to join the crusades to free the Holy Land from infidel Saracens. Furthermore, eleventh-century France was pining for strong central government after four centuries of anarchy since the death of the real Charlemagne; and a wise, powerful and paternal ruler was a very attractive ideal.

Moral

The moral is that, in order to understand a legend, it is often important to consider the period in which it grew and became widely known, as well as, or even more than, the period in which the events are supposed to have happened.

THESEUS AS A NATIONAL HERO

The evidence for the growth and popularity of Greek legends comes mainly from paintings on pottery, and from poetry. There are very early pictures of heroes (or gods) killing bull-headed men, which may, or may not be, Theseus killing the Minotaur; and there are pictures of a man and a woman boarding a ship, which may be Theseus and Ariadne, or Paris and Helen, or neither couple. What is evident is that the story of the labours of Theseus, that is to say his killing of the bandits on the road from Troezen to Athens, as well as the killing of the Minotaur, became a very popular subject in the sixth century BC.

Now one of the constant features in the history of classical Greece was the rivalry between the Dorian cities and the Ionian cities. The Dorians claimed to be descended from Herakles: and the invasions of Greece which destroyed the Mycenaean palaces were always known as the return of the descendants of Herakles. The leading Dorian state was Sparta. The leading Ionian state was Athens, and the Athenians claimed to have inhabited Attica since the Flood (see p. 73).

The sixth century saw the beginnings of Athenian democracy. If Athens was the one Mycenaean city which, though attacked, was never sacked (as Athenian legend related) then it is not surprising that the Athenians had a legend about the remote civilisation of Crete. That this legend was connected with a hero who was also located at Troezen is not surprising, as Mycenaean heroes frequently transferred themselves from one city to another – and may have done so in real life. That out of these elements the Athenians should have created for themselves a national hero who rivalled the Dorian Herakles as a benefactor to mankind, and displayed the qualities most admired in democratic Athens, is not surprising either, when we see what the English managed to do with Arthur, and the French with Charlemagne. Nor is it very surprising to find Theseus rising from the grave to help the Athenians in their hour of need at Marathon, driving the Persians back as he charged fully armed into their ranks.

ATTILA AGAIN

We have seen how, in the *Nibelungenlied*, an all but invulnerable dragon-slaying hero from a quite separate epic story has been woven into a plot which contains the historical characters Gundaharius the Burgundian, Attila the Hun, and his wife Ildico. In the same story appears Dietrich von Bern, who is none other than Theodoric the Goth, whose capital was Verona (Bern), and who ruled Italy after the deposition of the last Roman Emperor. Theodoric was born *after the death of Attila*.

The moral of this is that we cannot be assured that the nearly invulnerable Achilles, son of a goddess and invincible in battle, Agamemnon, the lord of golden Mycenae, Hector and Paris, sons of Priam and seventh in descent from Zeus, ever met together outside the walls of windy Ilion in combat over the possession of the most beautiful woman in the world, who was hatched out of an egg.

Legend and History

Historical understanding – the ability to project oneself in imagination into the past, and to think critically about how past events could have happened, and perhaps did happen – is a very sophisticated achievement of the human mind, which was attained by only a few Greeks in the classical period and not at all before the fifth century BC.

However, in any society the past *is there*: tangibly in the form of ruins, or the handiwork of artists and craftsmen which has survived destruction; and intangibly in customs and institutions whose origins are forgotten. Legends relate the present to the past and help to give the lives of those who tell and listen to them a meaning and purpose.

Legends are the product on the one hand of memories passed on from generation to generation (and among people who do not use writing memories are more precise and tenacious) and on the other of the experiences, and the hopes and fears, that each generation brings to the interpretation of those memories. Thus Arthur is an early medieval emperor in the writings of Geoffrey of Monmouth, a splendid example of late medieval chivalry in Malory's *Morte d'Arthur*, an idealised Renaissance prince in Spenser's *Faerie Queen*, and the perfect Victorian gentleman in the poetry of Tennyson. Whether or not there was ever a *real* King Arthur, or a *real* King Theseus, neither could have been anything like his legendary namesake.

Oedipus of Thebes

The city of Thebes was founded by Kadmos, a Phoenician prince, with the help of five men who had sprung from the sowing of a dragon's teeth. The early history of Thebes is full of fascinating incident, which must be omitted so that we can pass on to the seventh ruler, Laios.

Laios spent his youth in exile at the court of Pelops, where, as we have seen (p. 36), he fell in love with Chrysippos. After the death of Chrysippos he married Jocaste. An oracle had foretold that if he had a son that son would kill him; so when Jocaste gave birth to a boy, Laios ordered him to be exposed on Mount Cithaeron to die. However, the shepherd who received these instructions took pity on the baby and gave him to another shepherd who took him down the other side of the mountain, where he was adopted by Polybos, the childless king of Corinth, and named Oedipus because of his swollen feet.

Oedipus did not know that he was adopted; so, on growing up, he was puzzled and indignant when sneered at by one of the young men at court for his obscure birth. He therefore went to the oracle at Delphi to find out the truth. As soon as he crossed the threshold of the oracular shrine, the priestess ordered him to depart at once, as he was polluting holy ground, being a man destined to kill his own father and marry his own mother.

Horrified at this prophecy, he determined never to return to Corinth, still believing that King Polybos and Queen Periboia were his parents. Instead he turned in the other direction and came to where the road, passing alongside a precipice, is joined by another road. Here he encountered a fierce old man being driven in a chariot. The old man ordered him out of the way, and, when he resisted, struck him savagely with his goad. Oedipus was in no mood to be bullied and so he struck back and killed the old man and three of his servants. The fourth servant escaped. He happened to be that same shepherd who had been ordered to expose Oedipus.

OEDIPUS AND THE SPHINX

Proceeding on his way Oedipus eventually came to Thebes, to find it beleaguered by the Sphinx – a terrifying monster with the wings of an eagle, the body and limbs of a lioness, and the head of a woman. This monster asked a riddle which she had learnt from the Muses.[1] Anyone who gave the wrong answer she throttled and ate. Oedipus got the answer

[1] The Sphinx's riddle – 'What is it that goes on four legs, two legs and three legs, has one voice, and is weakest when it has most legs?' – has been asked as far afield as Mongolia and Central Africa.

Oedipus thinking out the answer to the Sphinx's question

right; whereupon she was driven by rage and humiliation to throw herself off the cliff where she sat, dashing herself to pieces on the rocks below.

OEDIPUS AND JOCASTE

The Thebans had promised to reward anyone who should rid them of the Sphinx with the kingship and the hand of the queen in marriage. These happened to be at their disposal because their previous king, Laios, had disappeared while on a mission to Delphi, murdered, so rumour said, by a band of robbers. So Oedipus became king and married the late king's widow. They had four children, and for several years he ruled wisely and successfully. However, the unlucky Thebans were once again visited by misfortune. This time it was a double affliction of both plague and famine. When consulted, the Delphic oracle declared that the cause was the failure of the Thebans to punish the murderer of their former king. So Oedipus, who, like all Mycenaean monarchs, was both king and high priest, solemnly pronounced a curse on the unknown murderer of Laios, and ordered all Thebans to disclose anything they knew about his death.

Eventually, with the help of the blind prophet Teiresias, the terrible truth was revealed. Both for Oedipus and for the Thebans, ignorance was no excuse; and his presence in the city was a source of defilement, certain to bring further disaster. So Oedipus went into exile, but not before Jocaste had hanged herself in shame, and he himself had put out his own eyes, because he could no longer bear to see the evidence of his unconscious crimes.

After years of wandering the roads of Greece as a blind beggar, accompanied by his loyal daughter Antigone, he came to Athens. There he was treated kindly by Theseus, and given, on his death, an honoured burial in the grove of Kolonos about a mile and a half from the city, where his bones would magically protect the Athenians against the Thebans who had cast him out.[1]

VARIANTS OF THE STORY OF OEDIPUS

That was, in outline, the story of Oedipus as told by the tragedian Sophocles. Owing to the popularity of his plays, and also to the theories of the founder of psychoanalysis, Sigmund Freud, it is often assumed to be the only version. In fact it is merely one of many treatments of the myth.

The *Iliad* refers to Oedipus once in lines which imply that he died violently, and was buried at Thebes. The poet of the *Odyssey* states that Jocaste (whom he calls Epicaste) married, in ignorance, her own son Oedipus, and, when the truth became known, hanged herself 'bequeathing many sorrows' to Oedipus; who nevertheless 'continued to rule over the Kadmeans in lovely Thebes'.

Hesiod mentions the Sphinx (whom he calls the Phix, meaning 'the throttler') as being the 'bane of Thebes', but his surviving works say nothing about Oedipus himself. References to early, but now lost, poems about Oedipus and Thebes show that these gave Oedipus no children by Jocaste, but made him marry a second wife, Euryganeia, who became the mother of his four children. There may have been a political reason for this: several aristocratic Dorian families traced their descent from Oedipus, and no doubt preferred to have a family pedigree that did not include incest.

However, Athenian writers would have no inhibitions about besmirching Dorian pedigrees; so possibly it was at Athens that Jocaste was first given four children by Oedipus. At any rate in the three plays that Aeschylus wrote about Oedipus this is the case. These plays, as far as can be conjectured from the one surviving play, treated the story as the tragedy of a family haunted, like the Tantalid family, by a curse. The curse may have been brought on Laios because he abducted Chrysippos; at least he was warned three times by the Delphic oracle not have a son.

---

[1] Perhaps they did. There is a possibility that a squadron of Athenian Cavalry defeated a squadron of Theban cavalry near the grove of Kolonos during the Peloponnesion War, when the Athenians were hard pressed and the Spartan king had led an invasion of Attica.

When he disobeyed, it led to his murder, to the incest and then to a further curse – the curse which Oedipus called down on his two sons Eteokles and Polyneikes, driving them to kill one another in a quarrel over which of them should succeed to the rule of Thebes. All of which illustrates, first, how free the Athenian tragedians were to alter myths to suit their artistic purposes, and, secondly, how difficult it is to be certain how far any particular version of a Greek myth is the invention of a particular writer remoulding old stories to suit his artistic purpose, and how far it is a genuine myth, developed spontaneously by a social group.

Note

The Great Sphinx of Gizeh (near Cairo) is the oldest sphinx to survive intact. It is seventy feet high and a hundred and fifty feet long, and wears the headdress of a Pharaoh on its human head. It was probably built about 2800 B.C. to symbolise the divine majesty of the Pharaoh as associated with the sun-god. It faces the rising sun. It is male and wingless. Female sphinxes with wings first appear in the art of Syria. Other sphinxes, pegasuses, chimairas and gorgons are found in the art of the Hittites, the Assyrians and other pre-Greek civilisations of the Near East. The sphinx illustrated here is a bronze ornament made about 550 B.C.

4
Folk-tales

Perseus

A MIRACULOUS BIRTH

PERSEUS was the grandson of Akrisios, King of Argos. Akrisios had been told by an oracle that he would be killed by the son of his daughter, Danae: so he constructed an underground chamber, put Danae into it, and set a guard over her. However, Zeus changed himself into a shower of gold and found his way to her through the roof; with the result that she conceived and gave birth to a son, Perseus.

A MIRACULOUS ESCAPE

Akrisios refused to believe that it was Zeus who had fathered Perseus; so he took mother and child and put them into a coffin-shaped box, and had them thrown into the sea. The box, however, floated, and was carried along by wind and waves until it was washed ashore on the island of Seriphos. Here Danae and Perseus were found and taken care of by a fisherman named Diktys, who happened to be the brother of the king of the island, Polydektes.

AN IMPOSSIBLE TASK

In time Polydektes fell in love with Danae, who did not respond to his passion. Thinking that it might be easier to get what he wanted if Perseus – who was now a fine young man – were out of the way, Polydektes pretended to be a suitor for the hand of Hippodameia (see p. 34), and asked his friends for contributions towards a wedding present for her. Perseus was delighted to see Polydektes taking an interest in someone other than his mother, and was tricked into promising to contribute the head of Medusa. Medusa was one of three Gorgons. Her two sisters were immortal, but she was mortal. They all had golden wings, scaly heads like dragons, tusks and brazen hands. Anyone who looked at them was turned into stone.

Athena and Hermes came to Perseus' help. They took him to the three Graiai, sisters of the Gorgons. These were old crones who had between them only one eye and one tooth, and they alone knew the way to the Stygian nymphs. By seizing their one eye and one tooth, Perseus blackmailed them into giving him the necessary directions. The Stygian nymphs possessed a cap which made the wearer invisible (Jack the Giant-killer had a coat of this material, which he called his 'Coat of Darkness'), and winged sandals ('Shoes of Swiftness'), and a magic wallet into which he could put the Gorgon's head. When he had borrowed these, he was given by Hermes a sickle of unyielding steel ('Sword of Sharpness'). Athena showed him how to approach the Gorgons while they were asleep, looking only at their reflections in a polished shield. With the help of the magic sickle he cut off Medusa's head, and with the help of the magic cap and sandals he escaped from the two immortal Gorgons, who had risen into the air to avenge their sister.

Perseus escaping with the head of Medusa in his magic wallet

A ROMANTIC ADVENTURE

On his way home via Ethiopia, Perseus came by chance upon the lovely Andromeda, chained to a rock and waiting to be eaten by a sea monster.

This had been sent as a punishment for the rash boast of Andromeda's mother, Kassiopeia. Kassiopeia had claimed that she was more beautiful than the Nereids, and Poseidon, angry on their behalf, had sent both a flood and a monster. Only the sacrifice of Kassiopeia's beautiful daughter – so the oracle of Zeus proclaimed – could appease the monster. Perseus instantly fell in love with Andromeda and promised her unhappy parents that he would extricate them from their predicament in return for the hand of Andromeda in marriage. The terms were agreed, and, with the help of his magic weapons, Perseus killed the monster and released Andromeda. This exploit bears a remarkable resemblance to Herakles' later rescue of Hesione (see p. 30); and, like Herakles, Perseus was nearly cheated of his reward. But, discovering in time the plot that Andromeda's uncle was hatching, he showed him Medusa's head and turned him into stone. He then continued on his way, taking Andromeda with him.

WICKEDNESS PUNISHED AND VIRTUE REWARDED

He arrived back at Seriphos in the nick of time. Polydektes was attempting to take Danae by force, and his threats had caused her and her protector Diktys to seek asylum in the temple of Athena. So Perseus showed Polydektes the objects he had been asked to fetch, and petrified him also. Having replaced him on the throne by his just and kindly brother Diktys, he set off for Argos, taking both Andromeda and Danae with him. But first he gave the magic weapons to Hermes to return to their owners; and the Gorgon's head he gave to Athena, who put it in the middle of her shield.

DESTINY FULFILLED

His grandfather Akrisios did not wait for his coming, but fled to Thessaly, hoping in this way to escape the fulfilment of the oracle. Perseus happened to go to Thessaly shortly afterwards to compete in some games. Taking his turn in the discus-throwing event he made a powerful throw, but the discus was deflected by a sudden gust of wind and fell just where Akrisios had the bad luck to be standing. He was killed instantly, thus becoming one of a distinguished company of fathers, grandfathers and uncles who found that it is impossible to cheat an oracle. Ashamed to succeed to the throne of someone he had accidentally killed, Perseus swapped Argos with his cousin Megapenthes for the cities of Tiryns and Mycenae, where he ruled successfully and became the grandfather of Eurystheus and Herakles. At this point, some would say, he emerges from the realm of folk-tale into the realm of legend.

Folk-tales

In Chapter 1 we sketched the distinctions that have been drawn between folk-tale, legend and myth, and found them difficult to apply. A teacher, when asked why her pupils enjoyed listening to Greek myths, replied, 'They just see them as super stories'. This answer is akin to the view that folk-tales are just enjoyable stories with nothing serious to say; but, as an answer, it prompts the further question: 'What makes a super story super?' – which is not at all an easy question. If it were, super stories could, presumably, be manufactured on demand according to formula.

One ingredient of many folk-tales is a logically neat and psychologically realistic solution to an unreal problem ingeniously posed. For example: given that there are one-eyed man-eating giants, what situation can you get yourself into that requires a solution of maximum ingenuity? Answer: together with twelve companions you are shut up in a cave with him, within earshot of his neighbours, by a boulder which he can, but you cannot, shift. (For the solution, see *Odyssey* Book IX.) Or: given that princes can be turned into animals by a spell, and released only when, without revealing their identity, they are granted three wishes by a young girl, how do you get the maximum psychological shock out of your plot? (*a*) What is to be your animal? (*b*) What are to be the three wishes? (*c*) How will they come to be granted? Answer: (*a*) A slimy frog: (*b*) 1. To sit by her at table; 2. To eat off her plate and drink out of her cup; 3. To get into her bed; (*c*) Exacted as the fulfilment of a promise thoughtlessly made in return for a trivial service (see *Grimm's Fairy Tales* no. 1, 'The Frog Prince').

Another ingredient of a good folk-tale is its power of symbolism: that is, its ability to suggest far more than it actually says.

THE BROTHERS GRIMM (1785–1863 and 1786–1859)

The first scholars to study seriously and scientifically the tales which were still being told by humble people were the brothers Wilhelm and Jacob Grimm, the editors of *Grimm's Fairy Tales*.[1] They began collecting folk-tales during the Napoleonic wars, and their intention was not to provide the nurseries of the well-to-do all over Europe with entertainment for their children – though this was one of the results of their labours – but to record what they considered to be a precious item of German national culture at a time when Germany was being overrun by the armies of

---

[1] The derivation of the word 'fairy' is significant when one considers the role of fairies in fairy stories. It comes through Old French from *Fata* (the Fates), the Latin equivalent of the Moirai, who spun the destinies of all human beings.

Napoleon. The work of the Grimms stimulated other scholars in other countries to begin collecting *their* folk-tales before it was too late.

It very nearly was too late, because the folk-tales had been passed on from one generation to the next by story-telling. Story-telling took place in country cottages after dark, when little else could be done; in lonely farmhouses, where the itinerant tailor came to stay to make clothes for the whole household, bringing his stock of stories with him; in the kitchens of the town houses, where peasant women brought country produce and stayed to tell a story in return for refreshment; in the small village work-shops, where the story-teller was sent for to beguile the women as they worked at the looms; and to the children in the big houses, by their peasant-born nurses, who had heard them in *their* childhood. But all through the nineteenth century, the art of story-telling was dying out, killed by the spread of literacy and the habit of reading, by the factory system and by the invention of strong artificial light.

Other Germans before the Grimms had been interested in their popular tales, and had woven them into poetry and fiction, just as the Greeks took tales, such as that of Perseus, for the themes of poems or plays on the killing of the Gorgon, on the peril of Danae with her baby in her floating chest, or on the rescue of Andromeda. In several countries collections of tales had been published by authors who had skilfully adapted the plots to the taste of well-bred audiences of their own day. Thus Italy had Boccaccio's *Decameron*, France *Cent Nouvelles Nouvelles* and the *Thousand and one Nights' Entertainment* (*The Arabian Nights*), which had been circu-lating round the cities of Baghdad, Damascus and Cairo for many years before they were written down by a Frenchman, translated and brought to Paris in 1701. Four years earlier had appeared *Stories and Tales of the past, with moral reflections*, by C. Perrault. These included such familiar favourites as *Cinderella*, *The Sleeping Beauty*, *Puss-in-Boots* and *Bluebeard*. They were charmingly written for the pleasure of the great ladies of the court of Louis XIV, and embellished with a moral in verse. But where had their author got them from? Probably, though not certainly, from peasant story-tellers of his day. If he did, he refashioned them to suit his audience.

MIGRATION OF FOLK-TALES

What was original about the work of the brothers Grimm was that they did not refashion, but wrote down the stories as they were told; for they considered that exact details were significant.

They believed their stories to be the 'debris of old Germanic religious belief'; that is to say, they thought that religious myths had 'degenerated', first into legends, and then into popular tales told purely for amusement. Subsequent study by folklorists and students of mythology who followed in the Grimms' footsteps showed that they were wrong about this. Though the tales have a style, setting and characterisation which relate them to the locality where they were collected, nevertheless the basic plots, in one variation or another, are to be found all over the world. Whether the stories have been passed on by travellers from one country to another, or whether they have been independently created through some common structure of the human brain, is yet another question that has not been decided. Some parallel tales are found so far afield that a common origin seems unlikely, if not impossible; but there is much evidence to show that a vast number of folk-tales have been circulating for many centuries, passing backwards and forwards from India to the West, from the Mediterranean to the Baltic, from the Celts of Ireland and Wales to the Slavs of Eastern Europe, out of one language and into another, and from popular tale into literature and back into popular tale again.

FOLK-TALE THEMES IN GREEK MYTH

In ancient Greece there were no folklorists to record popular tales in peasant cottages. If there had been, this chapter would have had to be much longer than it is. Though Greek civilisation was an urban civilisation – it grew up in the cities and thrived in the cities – yet the vast majority of Greeks lived in the countryside, and no doubt told many fairy tales just as Greek peasants do today.

Not having these fairy tales, we can only note the similarity of many episodes in Greek myths and legends to folk-tales which have been recorded since folklore became a subject for study by scholars. The adventures of Perseus have obvious parallels, so of course has the wooing of Thetis and her return to the sea. Similarly with Oedipus. Heroes who murder their fathers and marry their mothers are found in Finland, the Ukraine and Java. As for the disagreeable goddess whom no one invited to the wedding of Peleus and Thetis, but turned up uninvited in order to make trouble, she bears so striking a resemblance to the wicked fairy who ruined the christening of the princess in *The Sleeping Beauty* that it seemed unnecessary to point this out.

The *Odyssey* is full of fairy stories. It has seductive witches (Calypso and Circe); ogres and ogresses (Polyphemos and the giant man-eating Laestrygonians, and Scylla and Charybdis); a fairy godmother (Athena); a magic bag (the bag of the winds given to Odysseus by Aiolos) which brings ruin on Odysseus' shipmates through their curiosity and greed; a faithful wife who tricks her tiresome suitors by postponing her answer until she has finished weaving a shroud which she unpicks every night.

A Latin novel and a Greek fairy tale

The Sleeping Beauty, Puss-in-Boots and *Bluebeard* are examples of successful attempts to retain the simplicity of folk-tales, while adapting them to the taste of sophisticated readers. We have one Greek fairy tale of this kind. It *is* a Greek tale, although it appears in a Latin novel written in the second century AD by a North African whose home town was Madaura (in modern Tunisia).

The action of the novel is set in Thessaly (Northern Greece). A young man gets involved with a Thessalian witch. He tries to turn himself into a bird, but only succeeds in turning himself into an ass. In this shape he has many adventures, alarming, humiliating, shocking and funny, before he can find the rose petals he needs to eat in order to turn himself back into human form. Early in the story he is captured by brigands and taken to a cave, where they shortly afterwards bring a girl they are holding to ransom. The brigands go off again for more plunder, leaving the girl and the ass in the care of an old peasant woman. To quieten the girl, who cannot stop weeping and bewailing her misfortunes, the old woman tells what she calls 'an old wives' tale'.

The Greek Fairy Tale

'There were once upon a time a King and a Queen who had three lovely daughters: of whom the two elder, though beautiful, were not so beautiful that you and I could not find words to praise them; but the youngest. . . .'

The youngest is so beautiful that all the world comes to admire and adore her, which causes a double misfortune. In the first place, no man can bring himself to regard such a divinely lovely creature as a suitable wife for a flesh-and-blood husband; so she stays unmarried while her sisters find eligible husbands for themselves. Secondly, and much worse, the temples of the Goddess Venus are neglected and her anger aroused. She sends her son Cupid to punish Psyche by making her fall in love with the most repulsive and benighted mortal alive; but instead – so lovely and charming is Psyche – Cupid, the god of Love himself, falls in love with *her*.

Meanwhile Psyche's father has been told by an oracle that he must abandon her, dressed in mourning clothes, on a rock where she is to become the bride of a terrible and potent dragon. Weeping and sorrowing, he leads her to the rock, and leaves her there to await the fearful beast; but no beast comes. Instead Psyche is wafted by the winds to a magic palace where she is waited on by invisible servants, and visited in the darkness of the night by a lover whom she may touch and hear but is forbidden ever to see. Her happiness would be complete, were it not for the loneliness she feels during the daytime, and she longs for the company of her sisters. Again and again her invisible lover warns her against them, but she cajoles him into letting them visit her. They wheedle her secret out of her, and from jealousy set about persuading her that her lover must be a fearful monster whom it is her duty to kill. At last she is convinced, and goes to bed armed with a lamp and a sharp razor, both of which she conceals close at hand. She waits until her lover has fallen asleep, and then she prepares to cut off his dragon's head. But in the light of the lamp she sees, not a dragon, but the exquisitely beautiful form of the God of Love. In the emotion of the moment she spills a drop of hot oil from the lamp on to his shoulder. He wakes, and with bitter reproaches for her disobedience and faithlessness, he abandons her.

Poor Psyche wanders in misery seeking him, until she is eventually brought to Venus. Venus tortures her, and sets her five impossible tasks; which, with the aid of a swarm of ants, a talking reed, an eagle and a talking tower, she nevertheless accomplishes. The lovers are reunited; Psyche is made immortal and married to Cupid; and everyone lives happily ever after except for the two wicked sisters, who have brought about their own deaths by trying to waft themselves off the rock to the magic palace where Psyche had enjoyed the love of Cupid. Psyche, who has been pregnant throughout her torments, is delivered of a child 'whom we (mortals) call Pleasure'.

MORE THAN A FAIRY TALE

A fairy tale through and through. But the author, Apuleius, by giving the heroine the name of Psyche (which means 'the soul') and by many small touches which recall the teaching of Plato about ideal love, has contrived to make the story not merely a fairy story, but also an allegory of the human soul in search of immortality; and by placing it at the centre of his novel he indicates that, though picturesque, humorous, fantastic and bawdy, the novel is nevertheless serious and religious in intention. It suggests a great deal more than it actually says.

BEAUTY AND THE BEAST

The story of Cupid and Psyche is very similar to the story of *Beauty and the Beast*, whose authoress, Madame Leprince de Beaumont, also took a folk-tale and turned it into an elegant fable.

Like Psyche, Beauty is entertained in a magic palace expecting to be eaten by a revolting beast. Like Psyche, she finds eventually that her beast is no beast but possessed of every charm that a pure-hearted maiden could wish for in a husband. Like Psyche, she very nearly has her happiness ruined by her sisters who are beautiful, but not nearly as beautiful as she is, and corrupted by malice and envy. In both stories, vice is as neatly punished as virtue is satisfyingly rewarded. Madame Leprince de Beaumont works her plot by the machinery of gothic fairy tales – good fairies and bad fairies, and transformation by spells – which does not differ very much from the machinery of pagan mythology employed by Apuleius. However, the message she seems to be conveying to us is not about the soul and its quest for immortality, but about principles of conduct between daughters and fathers, and girls and their lovers. Nevertheless the analytical psychologists (see p. 62), who delight in analysing the hidden meaning of these two tales, usually declare that both of them are *really* about the response of young girls to sex and marriage.

A WRESTLING-MATCH WITH DEATH

Finally a folk-tale about death. When Apollo's son Asklepios was killed by Zeus with a thunderbolt (see p. 76), Apollo was overcome with grief and anger. Not daring to revenge himself on Zeus, he instead killed the Cyclopes who had forged the thunderbolt. To expiate this deed he was required by Zeus to spend a year looking after the cattle of Admetos, King of Pherai. Admetos, unlike Laomedon in similar circumstances, treated his divine servant so well that Apollo determined to reward him as handsomely as possible. Discovering from the Fates that Admetos was due to die young, he made them drunk and then talked them into agreeing to allow Admetos to live to a ripe old age if anyone could be found willing to die in his place. When the time came, the only volunteer was his beloved and loving wife Alcestis.

Scarcely had she expired when Herakles, an old friend of Admetos, arrived at the palace on his way to fetch the man-eating horses of King Diomedes (his Eighth Labour). Admetos' manners were so perfect that he welcomed Herakles and gave orders that no one was to tell him that the palace was in mourning for Alcestis, lest he should feel obliged to look for hospitality elsewhere; and arranged that he should be entertained in a manner suitable to his status and appetite (which was enormous).

However Herakles accidentally learnt the truth and was so overwhelmed by the nobility of his friend's conduct that he left his meal and went off to waylay Thanatos (Death) as he came to fetch Alcestis down to Hades. Wrestling with him till his ribs cracked he forced him to surrender his prey, so Alcestis was restored to life, and to her husband.

In this story, as in several others, Herakles has the robust vulgarity of a folk-hero, and themes of the reward for kindness to a supernatural creature who is temporarily at a disadvantage, and of bargains with fate or death (or with the Devil, who comes, like Death, from the Underworld to claim his prey) are common in folk-tales. And typical of folk-tale is the very materialistic conception of death as a disagreeable old man who can be overcome by brute force. (The Grimms have a story of Death being so badly knocked about by a giant that he begins to worry whether he will survive to carry on his job, and what will happen to the world if he doesn't.) None the less the folk origins of the story did not prevent the poet Euripides from turning it into a sophisticated play about the egotism of men, the selfishness of old age (Admetos' father and mother flatly refuse to die for him), and the noble love of a wife for her husband and children.

Note
Gorgons' heads were a favourite ornament among the Greeks, and thought to be efficacious in frightening away enemies and averting magic spells. They are found on temples, city walls and household furniture.

5

Theories about Myth

More questions

WHY do we dream? Why do certain situations occur and recur again and again in our and other peoples' dreams, such as: that we are in a public place or at an important ceremony, and wearing quite the wrong clothes, or no clothes at all; that we are flying; or falling off a high cliff; or, like Alice in Wonderland, falling into a deep well. 'Do not fear the prophecy that you will marry your mother,' says Jocaste to Oedipus in Sophocles' *Oedipus the King*, 'for many men have done this in their dreams.'[1] Why do the aborigines of Australia say that all their myths happened 'in the Dreamtime'? Why do dreams often play an important part in myths?

Many people who write about myth are agreed that there is a connection between myths and dreams. There is less agreement as to what precisely the connection is. Some anthropologists would say that people use the symbolism they have learnt from their mythology in order to interpret their dreams, and that this is the only connection between them. Some psychoanalysts, however, go so far as to regard dreams and myths as simply two sides of the same coin. In considering modern theories about Myth, it will be convenient to start from the psychoanalysts; but first let us look at what the Greeks themselves had to say on the subject.

SOCRATES AND MYTH

In Plato's dialogue *Phaedrus* – which may or may not give a true picture of the real Socrates – we find Socrates mocking at people who waste their time trying to produce commonsense explanations of myths; such as that the story of the abduction of Oreithyia (daughter of a legendary king of Athens) by Boreas (the North Wind) originated from a fatal accident to

---

[1] Hippias, son of the Athenian tyrant Peisistratos, and Julius Caesar are both reported to have had this dream.

the young lady when she was playing rather too near to a precipice and got blown over.[1]

Modern scholars would agree with Socrates in dismissing explanations of this sort as over-simple; but they would not agree with him that myths are not worth studying, and least of all for the reasons he gives.

> As far as I am concerned, [he says] such explanations are amusing, but tedious, and I don't envy anyone who undertakes them, because once he has begun he will not be able to stop but will have to give reasons for the shape of the Centaurs and the Chimaira[2] and all the horde of Gorgons and Pegasuses,[3] and other impossible monstrosities: and this rather foolish scientific exercise will waste a great

The Chimaira

deal of time, which I cannot afford. The reason that I cannot afford the time is that I have not yet succeeded in knowing *myself* – which is what the inscription over Apollo's temple at Delphi tells me I must do. And as long as I don't know myself it seems ridiculous to enquire into other things. So I'm quite ready to accept the common

[1] In more recent times the cat part of the Dick Whittington story has been 'rationalised' as originating from a supposed merchant ship, belonging to Sir Richard, named *The Cat*.

[2] A creature part lion, part goat and part dragon, which was killed by the hero Bellerophon.

[3] Pegasus was a winged horse which sprang from the blood of the decapitated Medusa. Bellerophon was riding on Pegasus when he killed the Chimaira.

view, that Oreithyia was carried off by Boreas from a spot just near here; and I propose to direct my researches, not into that sort of inquiry, but into myself, to find out whether I'm like Typhon – only more complicated and more passionate; or whether I'm a milder and simpler creature, endowed with a divine, modest and untyphon-like nature.

Many modern mythologists would think that, so far from being a waste of time, research into myth might achieve just what Socrates wanted to achieve: that is to say, it could help us to know ourselves by revealing truths about the working of our minds; truths which would not be revealed by the logical and analytical discussions which were Socrates' method of enquiry.

Typhon

How much truth has already been revealed by researches into myths (and dreams) is disputable; but with regard to Socrates' problem – whether he was *by nature* (*a*) Typhon-like, or (*b*) mild and divine – present opinion among psychologists seems to tend very much in the direction of (*a*) rather than (*b*).

Typhon, it should be explained, or Typhoeus – originally they were two separate monsters, but by the time of Socrates they had come to be considered as one – combined the destructive elements of whirlwind (or typhoon) and volcanic eruption. Thus Typhon is said to be the father of gales, and to be buried under Mount Etna, whence he sends up billowing clouds of smoke. He was buried under Etna by Zeus after a terrible battle, in which he very nearly got the upper hand and all but drove the gods from Olympos. He had a hundred snake heads, each with a dark flickering tongue; his two hundred eyes blazed fire; and his hundred mouths emitted each a different but fearsome noise: bellowing, roaring, hissing, barking or uttering speech intelligible (but alarming) to the gods.

Sigmund Freud (1856–1939)

The monster Typhon, as imagined in Greek mythology, is not altogether unlike that part of the human personality which Freud labelled 'the Unconscious'. Like the volcanic Typhon it is buried out of sight, but causes eruptions (in our personalities) and, like Typhon it is by nature violent, passionate and lustful, and not at all mild and divine. Divinity plays no part in Freud's theories, which are strictly biological.

Perhaps the first thing to grasp is that to the psychoanalysts (that is Freud and his followers) the new-born baby is not the innocent little angel idealised by sentimentalists, but a completely egotistical bundle of powerful biological cravings, which are there to help it fulfil its biological purposes of survival, and eventually procreation: and this bundle is highly vulnerable and helplessly dependent on its mother, father or any other adults who are available to protect and feed, warm and comfort it. Its cravings generate a high degree of energy whose natural outlet is acts of possessiveness and aggression directed towards adults, especially parents, who satisfy, fail to satisfy, or thwart its cravings; towards brothers or sisters who compete with it for the attention of adults; and towards its own body as the source of its sensations. While still tiny infants, we discover that attempts to satisfy some of our cravings produce reactions from adults that are painful to us, either physically or emotionally; and, to protect ourselves from these painful reactions, we 'repress' such cravings into our Unconscious, and redirect the energy into some substitute activity. But, though buried in the Unconscious, these cravings still affect our lives in adulthood, and direct much of our behaviour, and are responsible for many of our apparently chance accidents, slips of the tongue, lapses of memory, dreams and neurotic symptoms. From the feelings of passionate possessiveness of the male infant towards his mother, and his jealousy of his father, comes the 'Oedipus Complex' ('Why,' asked Freud, 'has the myth of Oedipus such compulsive interest for human beings?' Answer: because we have all repressed into our Unconscious the desire to possess our mothers, and, out of jealousy, to kill our fathers); and from the female infant's possessiveness towards her father and jealousy of her mother comes the 'Electra Complex' (for Elektra see page 37).

MYTHS

The telling of myths, according to Freud, is a disguised means of talking about certain important fantasies which we all have, though we are not consciously aware of them. These unconscious fantasies he calls the 'Racial Unconscious', which we all share alike, whereas each of us has our own individual Unconscious. Freud thought that we inherit this 'Racial Unconscious' from a stage in human evolution when the human mind was still 'young and incompetent', and our ancestors went about – as some species of animals do now – in a horde dominated by a powerful male. This male was the father of the horde and kept all the women for himself and subjected all the younger males to his power. Eventually the younger males rebelled and killed and ate the powerful father. From this event Freud derived his theories of religious ritual (the younger males felt a profound remorse and devised the rituals as a form of atonement). Subsequently the young males (to prevent quarrels among themselves over their women) made rules that marriage could take place only with females from outside the tribe. As the result of these rules all societies have a strong irrational abhorrence for incest (an abhorrence which does not, of course, exist among animals).

Freud also thought that the story of Moses in the Old Testament concealed a similar murder (though he does not say the Israelites ate Moses), and a similar remorse.

DREAMS AND SYMBOLS

Dreams were of more interest to Freud than myths, and his theories about them are much more impressive. He called dreams 'the royal road to the Unconscious': but it is a road along which only the trained psychoanalyst can successfully find his way, because he alone knows how to interpret the symbols which our Unconscious uses to communicate with us through dreams. These symbols allow us to express wishes about matters which we have been taught to consider shocking, but in such a way that the real nature of the wish is not apparent: otherwise we should be shocked at ourselves and wake up. According to Freud, dreams (or myths) about kings and queens are really about fathers and mothers; chests, caves and hollow objects symbolise the female womb (both Danae's underground prison and the box in which she was cast adrift would, presumably, be symbolising her female creativity); sticks, swords or snakes symbolise the male sex organ: and so on.

A true anecdote

A small boy, who had been told that he was soon to have a baby brother or sister, became very possessive towards his mother, and difficult and tiresome in his behaviour. One of his naughty acts was to go to the kitchen, open the oven and turn the joint out on to the floor; then he went to the refrigerator, pulled out the pudding and turned that on to the floor too. This incident could have no significance at all: but, if you accept Freud's theories, it neatly illustrates the working of symbolism in the little boy's Unconscious.

Carl Gustav Jung (1875–1961)

The analytical psychologist[1] Jung began by collaboration with Freud, but later quarrelled with him, and ended by disagreeing profoundly.

---

[1] Freud and his followers called themselves 'psychoanalysts'; Jung and his followers, to emphasise their disagreement, called themselves 'analytical psychologists'.

Jung replaced Freud's theory of a 'Racial Unconscious' by a theory of a 'Collective Unconscious'. Jung's Collective Unconscious is, like the Racial Unconscious, shared by everyone, but it is different from it in nature and origin.

Freud was, on the whole, a pessimist. For him, man cannot escape his biological urges which are inevitably frustrated by society. The more complicated society becomes, and the higher its degree of civilisation, the more men and women will be frustrated and the more unhappy and neurotic they will become. Jung, on the other hand, was a qualified optimist.

THE COLLECTIVE UNCONSCIOUS

Jung believed that man's rational nature (in this he includes sane ways of *feeling* as well as of thinking), which enables him to live in co-operation with his fellow men, is, biologically speaking, a recent and precarious achievement. It is superimposed on a Collective Unconscious which is no further developed than is the Collective Unconscious of animals. In animals the Unconscious produces instinctual behaviour, such as the building of nests by birds (some of them quite unnecessarily elaborate), the dances of bees, the courtship displays of birds and animals, and so on. In man the Unconscious produces the tendency to self-expression in certain symbols (crosses and swastikas, labyrinths, and stone circles like Stonehenge, are all such symbols) or by certain mythological themes which Jung discovered in myths from all over the world; it also produces, in the case of mental disturbance, irrational and compulsive acts, either individual, as in cases of kleptomania, sex crimes, or suicide; or collectively, as in national acts of frenzy or cruelty such as occurred during the Nazi régime in Germany. The sanity and happiness both of individuals and of society depend on the delicate adjustment between the needs of the rational mind and the needs of the Unconscious, which (like Freud's Unconscious) can communicate only through the symbolism of dreams and myth. Jung's optimism is, therefore, dependent on the development of an understanding, through analytical psychology, of the Unconscious.

Anthropological theories

Speaking very generally, the depth psychologists (that is the psychoanalysts and the analytical psychologists) in their explanations of myth begin from the individual and his biological inheritance. For anthropologists the most important fact is that man is a social animal – as Aristotle put it. Man's most significant and powerful impressions derive from his membership of a social group.

THE 'EXPLANATION OF RITUAL' THEORY

Primitive religion was – and is, where it still exists – intimately connected with the emotions aroused by the feelings of solidarity with one another which the members feel at tribal gatherings. These emotions become connected with symbolic objects, which in turn become the focus for rituals. The rituals give rise to stories (the myths) which appear to explain the rituals (they don't *really* explain them in any scientific sense, any more than the story of Guy Fawkes *explains* why we light bonfires and set off fireworks on a particular night in early winter).

THE 'CHARTER' THEORY

According to this theory the purpose of the myths is to ensure respect for the customs of the tribe, the superiority of certain families or individuals, or for claims to territory by groups or individuals. There are many examples' of Greek cities and individuals using myths for these purposes. (For example, the Athenians claimed the island of Salamis on the grounds that, in the *Iliad*, the hero Ajax brought his twelve ships from Salamis and beached them alongside the Athenians at the siege of Troy.)

In a society which makes use of writing, disputes on such matters are, of course, referred to documents – charters and constitutions and the like – but in a society where communication is mainly by word of mouth, reference to a story which goes back to time immemorial, and involves the gods or heroes of the tribe, is an accepted method of settling disagreements, or justifying conduct.

Even more important than the settlement of disputes is the sanctity of supernatural origins which myth can give to the restraints which society imposes on the selfish desires and appetites of the individual. These restraints, in a primitive society, rigidly regulate conduct, and consist of: the system of tribal authority; the rules of inheritance and of barter; marriage customs and prohibitions (these are essential for the harmony, and therefore survival, of the tribe and must be powerfully enforced); the division of labour between the sexes; how women are to be treated; the customs of child-rearing; the rules for burial; and so on. Why, it may be asked, is this effected by telling stories rather than quite simply by commandments? The answer may be that it is an advantage for a primitive society to have its 'charters' imprecise and ambiguous. In this way there is room for differing interpretations to suit the changing circumstances of the tribe. It is also possible that the ambiguity and vagueness make the myths more psychologically powerful, in that it is not easy to argue against them.

THE 'STRUCTURALIST' THEORY

Another reason given for the use of myth to convey messages about human conduct within a society is that the message of the myth is received, not by the conscious mind (nor indeed by the psychoanalysts' Unconscious), but subliminally,[1] as the result, not of one story on its own, but of the accumulated transmission of several stories. It is as if a wireless operator, using a faulty set, were to send the same message several times, with the units of meaning differently arranged, and with different wording, so that in the end the distortions cancelled themselves out and the message got through. Thus to understand the myth of Oedipus it is necessary, according to this theory, to consider also all the other stories about Thebes – Kadmos and the dragon's teeth; Laios and Chrysippos; Eteokles, Polyneikes and Antigone, etc. – and the etymology of the kings' names. With these the anthropologist behaves rather as if he had a sheaf of faulty telegrams, all trying to say the same thing in different ways, and had now to analyse their 'structure' (that is the relationships between units of meaning). According to structuralist theory, what the anthropologist then finds is a message expressed in pairs of opposed terms (binary opposition), and that this message is about unexpressed contradictions in the society's beliefs and customs. The Oedipus myth, for example, turns out to be about the contradiction between the *belief* that human beings came originally from the earth, like plants, and the *knowledge* that human beings are born from the union of men and women.

RESOLVING CONTRADICTIONS

Most classical scholars are dissatisfied with this analysis of the Oedipus story; nevertheless there is something to be said for the idea that one of the uses of myth is to handle contradictions in a society's beliefs, and prevent the members from worrying too much about them. One might take the example of a child asking why, if God is good and all-powerful, do human beings have to die; and for an answer being told the story of the Garden of Eden. In this story there are the binary opposites of men and gods, heaven and earth, desert and garden, tree of life and tree of knowledge, man and woman, life and death. By eating from the tree of knowledge Adam and Eve come to know each other as man and woman, and so

[1] Like certain types of advertising which are supposed to affect the way you spend your money without your being aware of it.

can beget and conceive and have offspring, so that life will continue; but for eating the fruit they are banished from the tree of life and doomed to die. So the child's question has not received a logical answer – in matters of religion final answers in terms of logic are impossible – but has received a symbolic answer which is psychologically satisfying and, because the answer is presented as a story of something that happened, it can be used to discourage further questions 'why?' by the statement that this is how it was in time long ago and there is no more to be said.

It used to be felt that each new theory of myth necessarily superseded all previous ones. Some scholars now feel that the importance of myth to primitive, and not-so-primitive, societies may well be that it performs many functions at once. Thus the story of the Garden of Eden handles many other matters besides the contradictions in our beliefs about life and death. It gives sanctity to the institution of marriage, and to the superiority of husbands over wives. It 'explains' why humans have to work for their livelihood, and why childbirth is painful. Furthermore the story employs many of the Freudian symbols – trees, fruit, a serpent, a flaming sword – which could deepen its significance by affecting us at the level of our Unconscious.

*   *   *   *

A discarded theory

A number of theories about myth have been put forward in the past, and subsequently discarded. Only one of these need be mentioned: the theory that myth is a primitive and erroneous kind of science (mistaken explanations of natural phenomena, such as the seasons, storms, earthquakes and the like); and ritual a mistaken kind of technology (a futile attempt to control nature). This theory was abandoned when anthropologists went to live in primitive societies, and found that myths and rituals performed valuable social functions which had nothing to do with satisfying scientific curiosity, or with trying to control nature. It may be significant that this theory dates from the Victorian era when evolution and progress from the darkness of savagery to the light of nineteenth-century scientific rationalism seemed to be a self-evident fact. A hundred years and two world wars later, primitive man seems less primitive, and scientifically-minded rational men to be less in a position to patronise 'primitive' ways of life and thought.

Theories about the origins of Greek myths

The only other theories we need be concerned with are not about myth in general, but specifically about the origins of Greek myths. These are based on guesses about developments in religious worship in the prehistoric period of Mediterranean culture. The guesses arise from the study of statuettes, engravings on gems, and pictures on cups, weapons and palace walls, all recovered from the excavations of sites in Greece or the Greek islands (including Crete and Cyprus) which date from the period between 3000 BC and the coming of the Dark Age in about 1100 BC. Other information comes from documents written in the languages of the Hittites, Babylonians, Sumerians and other peoples of the Near East. Among other relevant clues, these documents contain religious poems and epics, such as those of Marduk and Gilgamesh, which show unexpected resemblances to the myths and epics of Greece.

THE MATRIARCHY THEORY

In its most extreme form this theory runs thus:

Before the arrival in the Eastern Mediterranean of Greek-speaking people, Mediterranean societies were dominated by their women. Religion consisted of the worship of a single goddess, or of several goddesses, conducted by priestesses. Originally the biological connection between sexual intercourse and child-bearing was not realised: winds and rivers were thought to be responsible for pregnancy. Even when the connection was realised, the status of men remained low. The tribal society was ruled by a woman; to men were delegated certain functions, such as hunting and herding and defending the territory of the tribe. The ruling queen took an annual consort, whom she ritually sacrificed at the end of each year.

The history of Greek religion, according to this theory, is the story of the intrusion into this Mediterranean society of Greek-speaking people from the north-east, who worshipped a male deity and whose society was dominated by its men. At first the intrusion was fairly peaceful. The leaders of the Greek-speakers married the reigning queens and gradually asserted *male* authority over *female*, and the superiority of their own *gods* over the pre-Greek *goddesses*. Eventually, with further invasions of patriarchal Greeks, the civilisations of Minoan Crete and Mycenaean Greece became entirely male-dominated, and religion became predominantly the worship of the patriarchal Zeus and his sons and brothers. Greek mythology, then, is the history, in allegorical terms, of the political and religious changes which took place between 2000 and 1000 BC. Stories of the rapes of nymphs by gods represent the marriages between Greek chieftains and local priestesses, and the story of the birth of Athena represents the replacement of the worship of the goddess Metis, the old goddess of wisdom, by Zeus as the new god of wisdom. (The story was that Zeus begot Athena on Metis by force, then swallowed Metis; Athena, at a blow from the axe of Hephaistos, sprang fully armed from Zeus' head.) Athena took over the temples of Metis, which were left undisturbed on the understanding that her worshippers accepted the sovereignty of Zeus.

This reconstruction is almost entirely guesswork, and present-day anthropologists are sceptical about the likelihood of a society totally dominated by its women. None the less there is archaeological evidence to support the theory that the pre-Greek civilization lived mainly by agriculture and worshipped goddesses of fertility, and was overrun by Greek-speaking people who were hunters, and herders of flocks, and worshipped male gods of the sky.

THE NEAR EAST

The theory that *all* Greek myths could have originated in this clash of cultures has been weakened by the recent realisation that Mycenaean Greece formed part of a common civilisation with many cities of Asia Minor, and that many themes and stories in Greek mythology probably came to Greece from Sumer, Babylon, Nineveh and Akkad, via the cities in Syria and the Lebanon and the Hittite Empire, with all of which the Mycenaeans had contacts through trade and diplomacy. The Greek story of Deukalion and Pyrrha and the Flood is an obvious example, as the Mesopotamian cities suffered disastrously from flooding, but Greek cities scarcely at all. So, unless one takes a psychoanalytical view that the flood is purely a symbol used by our Unconscious, it seems reasonable to doubt that such a myth would occur spontaneously in Greece or Crete.

The birth of Athena from the head of Zeus. Hephaistos has just relieved Zeus' headache by striking him with an axe

Note

The garment projecting from Athena's left shoulder is her *aegis*, a short goatskin cloak fringed with snakes and emblazoned with a Gorgon's head. It was worn only by Zeus and Athena (and occasionally by Apollo), and caused terror to their enemies.

6

'Pure' Myths

The functions of myth

WITHOUT committing ourselves too fully to any of the theories outlined in the last chapter we can say: that myths are a form of communication – though from whom, to whom, and what the precise message is in any particular case, must still remain in doubt; that they serve to make either the individual more psychologically comfortable, or a society more stable, by telling unreal and impossible stories, which take place outside time, about matters which are a source of concern to social groups in general or to particular social groups. The myth may include justifications for customs and beliefs, but these justifications will not be of a logical nature: the function of myth is to affect feelings, not thoughts; attitudes, not opinions.

In this chapter we shall look at some of the sources of concern which are revealed by the subject matter of Greek myths. These will be: the relationship between gods and men; death and its aftermath; the opposition between nature and society; and conflicts within the family.

Gods and men

Herodotus, writing in the fifth century, said:

> Whence each of the gods came, or whether they always existed, and what their appearance is, was unknown until yesterday, so to speak. For I think Homer and Hesiod lived four hundred years before me and not more; and they it was who composed for the Greeks the story of the creation of the gods, and gave these gods their names and defined the honours due to them, and the arts they controlled, and indicated their appearance (II, 53).

Hesiod called his creation story a *Theogony* (birth of the gods). Like Homer, he declares that he got his information from the Muses (the nine goddesses of artistic inspiration), which means, presumably, that he selected from already existing stories of unknown antiquity. How far he modified these stories is uncertain, but, whereas the authors of the *Iliad* and the *Odyssey* moved in aristocratic circles (or so it is conjectured from the nature of their poems), Hesiod was a peasant farmer who had suffered injustice at the hands of the rich (we know this because he tells us so); and his poems have a very unhomeric preoccupation with wickedness and injustice and their origins, and a pessimistic view of life on earth.

THE THEOGONY

In the beginning was Chaos (a gaping abyss). After Chaos came Gaia (Earth), Tartaros (the depths of the earth), and Eros (the sex instinct). From Chaos came Erebos (Darkness) and Nyx (Night), and from the union of Nyx and Erebos were born Aither (the upper air) and Hemera (Day). The children of Gaia include the hills, the sea, Okeanos (the river that flows round the world), Themis (law and order), Mnemosyne (memory), the Cyclopes, and various hundred-armed and fifty-headed giants.

This teeming brood of creatures is dominated by a succession of world-ruling gods, each of whom deposed his father by violence. First came Ouranos (Heaven), who begot innumerable children on Gaia, but hated them and buried them under the earth (Gaia herself). At last Gaia revolted and persuaded one of her children, Kronos, to castrate his father. So Kronos succeeded to the throne, and begot a host of children on his sister Rheia; but, because he knew that retribution was due to him for what he had done to his father, he swallowed them one by one as soon as they were born. Eventually Rheia, like Gaia before her, rebelled against the insufferable egotism of her husband and concealed her latest-born child, Zeus, giving Kronos a stone wrapped up in baby-clothes to swallow in his place. Zeus grew up concealed in a cave in Crete, became powerful and forced his father to disgorge his brothers and sisters, and then released his uncles whom Kronos had imprisoned. They, in gratitude, gave him the irresistible thunderbolts which assure his rule over all creatures, mortal or immortal. But before he could be secure on his throne he had to fight a stupendous war with the Titans (children of Gaia). For ten years the issue hung in the balance, but at last, with the help of three of Gaia's other children, the hundred-handed giants Briareos, Kottos and Gyes, he was victorious, and imprisoned the Titans under the earth for eternity. Having firmly established his rule, Zeus proceeded to apportion control over the various elements among his family and allies.

The families of the primal gods

These gods are divided into three families: the children of (1) Nyx;

(2) Ouranos and Gaia; (3) Pontos (sea). The children of Nyx kept themselves apart, the other two families interbred.

The children of Nyx included: the Moirai (the Fates: etymologically the ancestors of the fairies – see page 51n.); Nemesis (Doom); Apate (Deception); Geras (Old Age); and Eris (the goddess of Strife, who interfered in the wedding of Peleus and Thetis). Eris herself had children, a very disagreeable brood like herself: Toil, Forgetfulness, Famine, Battles and Lies.

Pontos was the father of Nereus, and so grandfather of Thetis and her forty-nine sisters. He was also grandfather to the Graiai and the Gorgons, and great-grandfather to the Chimaira and the Sphinx; all of whom are also descended from Gaia.

PANDORA'S BOX

The crimes of Prometheus, benefactor of mankind

In addition to the *Theogony* Hesiod wrote the *Works and Days*, a poem about farming addressed to his brother, who had cheated him out of his proper share of their father's farm. In both the *Theogony* and the *Works and Days* he tells, with slight variations, the story of Prometheus and Pandora. Prometheus was a Titan who had taken the side of Zeus in the ten-year struggle between gods and Titans. He had been rewarded by being admitted to the company of the gods on Olympos. He was always very friendly and helpful towards mankind – indeed, according to one story, which is not found in Hesiod, he had been given the task of creating them out of clay and then giving them to Athena, who breathed life into them. For the benefit of mankind Prometheus deceived Zeus. When it came to deciding how the sacrificial meat should be apportioned, Prometheus took the carcass and wrapped the bones in fat to make an inviting parcel, and so deluded Zeus into choosing that portion for the gods and leaving all the best meat for men. In annoyance Zeus took fire away from men, but Prometheus stole it back again from Olympos, concealing it in a hollow stalk. For this offence Prometheus was chained to a rock and had his liver eaten out every day by an eagle – it grew again at night so that it could be eaten out all over again next day. At last he was delivered by Herakles. Some writers (but not Hesiod) said this was in return for revealing the secret about the offspring of Thetis – that he was fated to be more powerful than his father – and so saving Zeus from marrying her and being deposed.

The first woman

As far as men were concerned, Zeus took his revenge by sending them women. He ordered Hephaistos to create a female. On her the gods lavished every gift of beauty, seduction and feminine accomplishment.

Hermes then gave her a 'deceitful and bitch-like mind'. Now Prometheus, whose name means 'Foresight', had a brother Epimetheus, whose name means 'Hindsight'. Prometheus had warned his brother to accept no gifts from the gods; but the latter, being Epimetheus, forgot and gladly took this irresistible creature whose name was Pandora ('Every Gift'). She had brought with her a jar (or box) in which all the gifts of the gods to man were enclosed. Since she was a woman, her curiosity got the better of her and she opened the box to look inside, and found that she had released all the diseases and evils that plague humanity, who had previously lived free from sickness and toil. So it is not only in *Genesis* that women get the blame for the sufferings of man and his need to work for his living.

The Flood

In the next generation Zeus found men altogether too presumptuous and so he sent a flood and destroyed them all except for Deukalion and Pyrrha, the son and niece of Prometheus, who had been warned by him to make an ark. They thus survived and were instructed by Zeus to create a new race of men by throwing stones over their shoulders.

COMMENT

Most mythologies include an account of fire and its origin; not surprisingly, since it is so important to primitive man. The story of the division of the sacrificial meat seems to refer to a mythical never-never period when gods and men feasted together – so perhaps does the story of Tantalos (see p. 34). The Flood story must be an importation from Mesopotamia. So it is possible that these are very old myths which Hesiod had difficulty in harmonizing with his theme that order developed out of chaos, and that the reign of Zeus represented the triumph of Law and Order in Heaven and a force for punishing the injustice which was still rife on earth. This may be why he implausibly relates that Zeus was not really deceived about the sacrificial meat, and that he consented to the release of Prometheus solely in order to increase the glory of Herakles.

Hesiod omits the tale of the Flood, and instead follows up with his account of the seven races of men, which goes roughly thus:

The Races of Men

The gods and men sprang from the same source. In the time of Kronos the gods made a golden race of men who lived like the gods themselves. These men knew no sorrow or hardship or old age: the earth gave them every fruit without toil; and when they died it was as if they had fallen asleep. After their death they roamed the earth as guardian spirits, giving wealth and keeping away evil.

F

After the golden race, the gods made a silver race of men, inferior in body and spirit. It took them a hundred years to grow up, but when they did they survived for only a short while, because they wronged one another, and refused to sacrifice to the gods. So Zeus was angry and buried them in the earth, where they remain as spirits of the underworld.

After the silver race Zeus made a bronze race of men. They were strong and violent; and their armour, their houses and their tools were of bronze – they had no iron. They spent their lives fighting, and so destroyed one another and went down to Hades, leaving no name behind them.

The bronze race was succeeded by a juster, better race of heroes, called demigods. Some of these were killed fighting for Thebes and some fighting for Troy, but others Zeus sent to dwell at the ends of the earth in the Isles of the Blessed. There they live happily under the rule of Kronos, whom Zeus released specially for this purpose.

After the age of the demigods comes the Iron Age. This is the age in which *we* are unlucky enough to be born. There are a few good things mingled with our evils, but the future is gloomy. The generations will hate one another (the 'generation gap'), and there will be no respect shown for old age, or for fair dealing. Might will be Right, and envy and perjury will drive Reverence and Righteous Indignation to flee from mankind and take refuge with the gods. Eventually children will be born precociously old, and Zeus will destroy our race too.

HESIOD'S MYTHOLOGY AND HOMER'S

All myth, as we have frequently had occasion to observe, is ambiguous and inconsistent; but Hesiod's stories contain more contradictions than most. This may be because he is trying to reconcile them with a moral sense which he has developed as the result of seeing and experiencing the effects of injustice. Homer, on the other hand, seems to have no such difficulties with the most outrageous behaviour on the part of his gods. In *Genesis* God created man in his own image. In Homeric mythology the gods have been created by man in the image of the aristocratic society of eighth-century Ionia, where the *Iliad* and *Odyssey* were composed.

THE NATURE OF THE HOMERIC GODS

Homer's gods are aristocrats living in an age when aristocrats enjoyed a monopoly of power and privilege. Heaven is a very exclusive club (predominantly a man's club – the goddesses, except for Athena, do not cut much ice there) run by a President who is not above employing violent measures when members dispute his authority. The members all possess superhuman powers and are immune from disease, old age and death. One of their chief characteristics is a jealous determination to have their superior status respected by mortals, whom they treat with feudal capriciousness, making free with their women, interfering in their affairs when the mood takes them, promoting favourites (but woe betide any who get above themselves!), implacable in revenge, and intimidating in their power and splendour. They recognise certain restraints, such as: (1) the overall pre-eminence of Zeus, whose power is in turn vaguely limited by the Fates – his occasional inclinations to set aside their decisions are greeted with hostility and reproach by the other gods; (2) the division of rule among themselves, decreed by Zeus, which they, on the whole respect; (3) a certain awe for the mysterious power of Hades, the god of the Underworld. Several of them have their own sphere of influence, or favourite locality, but all are frequently to be found on Olympos, feasting in unquenchable joy and merriment which is broken only by occasional quarrels. These arise from their jealousy of one another, or from their taking different sides in human affairs, as at Troy, or from Zeus' continual adulteries which sour his relations with his sister and consort, Hera. And from time to time there are stirrings of revolt against Zeus' authoritarianism.

The abode of the Gods

There is a Mount Olympos in Northern Greece, which is an awe-inspiring, cloud-capped peak; but the Greeks did not imagine that they needed only to make a long, stiffish climb up this to find themselves among the gods, any more than Christians have supposed that a balloon ascent would take them to Heaven. There were several other peaks called Olympos in Greece and Asia Minor, and these and other mountain tops had their altars to Zeus, who was naturally at home in such places, being a sky-and-weather god. However, after the time of Homer and Hesiod, Heaven (Ouranos) and Olympos are practically synonymous; and the comic poet Aristophanes, who exploited the satirical possibilities of an abode of the gods 'up there' by sending one of his characters to interview the gods riding on a giant flying dung-beetle, seems to have envisaged the palace of Zeus as in the sky, rather than on a mountain top. Hesiod, incidentally, reckoned that it would take a bronze anvil ten days to fall from Heaven to earth, and another ten to fall from earth to Tartaros, where the Titans were imprisoned.

Death and its aftermath

ODYSSEUS AND THE KINGDOM OF THE DEAD

On the subject of death Greek mythology was, by contrast with Egyptian mythology, vague and contradictory. We have already (p. 56) seen one folk-tale version of what happened to people after they died, but usually it was Hermes not Thanatos who was supposed to take the souls of the dead to the Underworld. Odysseus, in Book XI of the *Odyssey*, sought the land of the dead, and found it at the ends of the earth, beside the river of Okeanos. There he saw his mother, who told him:

> This is the law of mortal nature. When we die, we no longer have sinews to hold together our flesh and bones. They are consumed by the fierce heat of the funeral pyre when our spirit once leaves our white bones in death. Then our soul flits away like a dream [lines 218–22].

Odysseus saw the dead being judged and the wicked being tormented, and discovered that, even for the virtuous, death was a dim and dismal existence.

ORPHEUS

The story of Orpheus and his attempt to rescue Eurydike seems to emphasize the inevitability of death. Not even Orpheus, who could charm Charon, Kerberos and Hades himself, could succeed in conquering death. The very intensity of his love for Eurydike prevented him from keeping the bargain that he must not look behind him to see if she was following him up to the light.

ASKLEPIOS

That death is inescapable seems also to be the message of the story of Asklepios, son of Apollo. Under the tuition of Cheiron he became such a skilful healer that he could cure anyone; but he went too far and started bringing the dead to life (some say Hippolytos, others the seven heroes who died at Thebes). This caused Hades to complain that his rights were being infringed, so Zeus killed Asklepios with a thunderbolt.

DEMETER AND PERSEPHONE AND THE ORPHIC HYMNS

The myth of Persephone's descent into the underworld, and subsequent re-emergence for nine months of the year, was associated with religious rites celebrated at the village of Eleusis in Attica. Those who partook were sworn to secrecy, and the 'mystery' was so well kept that no one knows what happened in the rites or what doctrine they taught, but it is generally thought that they had something to do with a promise of a joyful life after death.

Hermes sits waiting to escort a dead woman to the Underworld

Note

The object in Hermes' left hand is his staff, given to him by his half-brother Apollo. It was a golden twig, branching into two shoots which have been twisted into an incomplete figure-of-eight. Some paintings and sculptures show the figure-of-eight as consisting of two entwined serpents. The staff is both a magic wand and a herald's staff, such as was carried by mortal heralds from Homeric to classical times, possibly derived from a symbol of authority carried by Mycenaean palace officials.

Similarly unknown to us is the content of the religious poems that were ascribed to the mythical Orpheus. Most likely they taught that the body is a prison for the soul; that life is a punishment for past sins; and that the soul can achieve salvation and release from its prison by a lifetime of abstinence – which includes vegetarianism; and that the souls of the dead can migrate into other living creatures.

GREEK IDEAS ABOUT DEATH

All in all the classical Greeks seem to have had very vague ideas about what happened to mortals when they died. But then so have we – if one may judge from the inscriptions on our gravestones, our funeral service and our custom of putting flowers on the graves of our loved ones.

*   *   *

MYTH AND RELIGION

This book is about Greek mythology not about Greek religion as a whole, which is the subject of another book in this series. For this reason we have used such phrases as 'god of the sea' and 'the Goddess of Marriage' without discussing difficult questions such as 'What did the word "god" mean to a Greek?' 'How did people come to believe that there were gods of the sea?' and 'What was a Goddess of Marriage thought to do for marriage?' Such discussion would have led to an inquiry into the remote origins of the gods to whom Homer and Hesiod gave shapes and characters – origins in the religious consciousness of the pre-Greek peoples of the Eastern Mediterranean, of the Greek-speaking invaders, and of the civilisations of the Near East (Sumer, Babylon, Nineveh and others) whose religious ideas spread westwards. It would also have led to a further discussion of how religious ideas developed within the framework of an existing mythology.

Myth, as we have observed before, is both ambiguous and adaptable. We can see that this is so even with Christianity, where there has always been an organised church to deter schism and heresy. The myths of Christianity – the Creation, the Garden of Eden, the Prophecy of Isaiah, Christ's Nativity and Resurrection – have provided a framework for religious beliefs as dissimilar as the Catholicism of the Crusades, of the Spanish Inquisition and of St Francis of Assisi, the Calvinism of the witch-burnings, the pacifism of many modern Christians, and so on. There being no organized church, new developments in religious thinking took place more easily in ancient Greece. The Zeus of Homer, who behaves like a larger-than-life epic hero, has no morals and cannot protect his mistresses from the jealousy of his wife, is a very different god in the plays of Aeschylus. In Aeschylus he is above all the guardian of Justice. In turn Aeschylus' Zeus has undergone a transformation by the third century BC, in the poetry of Aratos, to whom St Paul was referring when he said, preaching at Athens, 'In him we live and move and have our being; as certain also of your poets have said, for we are also his offspring'. An even more striking transformation took place with the hero Asklepios, whom we left a few paragraphs ago in Hades, whither he had been sent by a thunderbolt from Zeus. Towards the end of the fifth century BC the myth arose that he was revived and became the God of Healing in the place of his father Apollo. Shrines were built to him (the most famous at Epidauros) which became centres of healing and for seven centuries or more he was widely worshipped and regarded as the patron of all doctors.

Nature and Society

THE CYCLOPES

Man is an animal, and only by satisfying his animal instincts does he survive and propagate his kind. On the other hand he is more than an animal in that he can so communicate and co-operate with others of his kind in such a way that he forms not herds but societies and so immensely increases his power to manipulate nature to serve him. But this, in turn, makes him something less than an animal, in that wild animals are free from restraints to stop them satisfying their urges; whereas man, in order to live in society, must impose upon himself prohibitions against killing whom he wishes, mating with whom he wishes, and acquiring the property of other human beings as and when he wishes.

The Cyclopes may have interested the Greeks because they occupied an ambiguous place in the scheme of things, somewhere between beasts, men and gods.[1]

> The Cyclopes [the *Odyssey* tells us] do not have assemblies for taking council, nor any laws, but live in caves among the mountains, and each one lays down the law for his children and his wives [as does Freud's dominant male in the primal horde: see p. 61] and nobody pays any attention to his neighbours [IX 112–15].

They pasture sheep and goats and make cheese and drink wine; but they do not have to plant their vines or wheat or barley. Their land is a Garden of Eden where these things spring up of their own accord. They have no religion. 'We Cyclopes,' boasts Polyphemos, 'pay no attention to Zeus,

[1] On a less serious level Tarzan is interesting because he is envisaged as *both* civilised man *and* animal; less serious because the inherent contradictions are never thought out.

nor to the other blessed gods, since we are far stronger than they.' [IX, 275–6.] None the less they are not gods themselves, since they are mortal. Neither are they simply monstrous beasts, since they can talk and think and know the arts of domesticating animals. They are superior to men, in that they do not have to labour for a living, they can hurl rocks the size of mountains, and they can disregard the laws of Zeus with impunity. On the other hand, by comparison with men their technological level is low. They do not know how to make ships, and so cannot profit from the delectable island which lies just off their shores. And their rudimentary powers of co-operation quickly break down through misunderstanding, when Odysseus plays his crude 'No-man' trick.

THE CENTAURS

Another race of monsters who can be considered as existing somewhere between beasts and men are the Centaurs – half horse and half man. With the striking exception of Cheiron, they are wild and lecherous creatures, always eager to carry off human women, greedy for wine and prone to lose all control of themselves under its influence. Like Polyphemos they live in caves, but, unlike him, they are not cannibals.

The earliest representations of Centaurs show them as complete men with human arms, legs and body, but with the hindquarters of a horse attached. Later representations give them the complete body of a horse: that is, all four legs and body, with the torso, head and arms of a man attached where a horse has its neck. This arrangement lends itself to the allegorical interpretation of the Centaur as a creature whose human civilised nature is at the mercy of its powerful animal appetites – a point not lost on designers of modern advertising, who use them as symbols of virility.

Conflicts within the family

An eminent anthropologist has remarked that the message of a very large number of Greek myths and legends could be summed up thus: 'For the human race to continue it is necessary for fathers to be destroyed by their sons and betrayed by their daughters' – despite the fact that devotion to one's parents is considered a sacred duty. This is a contradiction at the core of human life and the source of much tragedy – and many Tragedies. Sooner or later the young males of each generation must displace the older generation (to be displaced in their turn by the next generation); and girls must abandon their parents and ally themselves with a male from outside the family and of the new generation.

A centaur

Kronos and Zeus set the pattern for sons dispossessing their fathers. Their example is followed by Oedipus and Theseus, while Jason and Perseus kill and dispossess their uncle and grandfather respectively.

DAUGHTERS BETRAY FATHERS

Ariadne, Medeia and Hippodameia all betray their fathers on behalf of handsome strangers, and so, in legends not referred to in this book, do Scylla and Komaitho.

WIVES BETRAY HUSBANDS

Klytaimnestra is the outstanding example; but Phaidra tried to seduce her stepson Hippolytos; Anteia, the wife of Proitos, tried to seduce her husband's guest Bellerophon: and in both cases the guilty woman put the blame on the innocent man. And, should you have been wondering what was so special about Peleus that he was selected to be the bridegroom of Thetis, his claim was based on his coming through a similar experience with Astydamia, the wife of Akastos, with his virtue unscathed.

FATHERS DESTROY SONS

Theseus killed his son Hippolytos by a curse, and Oedipus by a curse brought about the destruction of Eteokles and Polyneikes. Laios failed to destroy Oedipus, and Priam Paris, only because of the meddling of their servants.

Nor is this list of family crimes in Greek mythology anything like complete; so perhaps it is not surprising that Freud saw myths as the thinly disguised expression of guilty wishes created by stresses within the family.

Epilogue: Myth in Life, Literature and Art

Myth in sophisticated societies

WHAT happens to myths when they are no longer believed in?

This is a difficult and important question and it is beyond the scope of this little book to answer it adequately. Of course, if you asked it of a depth psychologist, you might get the answer that the question is misguided because your Unconscious will continue to 'believe' in the myths as much as it ever did, regardless of what your conscious mind may think.

If it had been asked of the Grimm brothers, on the other hand, they would have said that myths degenerated into legends and legends into folk-tales. But this answer would not satisfy most people because in many cases the development seems to have been in the opposite direction.

A third answer might be that the myths become so richly associated with the cultural traditions of a civilisation that they remain indispensable in helping its members to organise their perceptions of the events of their lives, and their responses to them.[1] The less tightly a society controls the behaviour of its members, the more frequently they are offered choices of

---

[1] *Organising perceptions and responses.* Seeing, hearing and feeling are not as straightforward as one might suppose if one never gave the matter much thought. In fact from birth onwards we learn (probably with the help of an inherited disposition, or 'set') to regard certain perceptions – of sights, sounds or feelings – as much more significant than others, while many sights, sounds and feelings we learn to ignore altogether. This begins with perceptions which we learn to recognise as warnings against pain (such as glowing red coals, steaming water or the tones of an angry voice) or as promises of pleasure (such as cooking smells or the voice of someone who is kind to us). As we grow up our training becomes much more subtle and complex, as we learn from other members of our society that certain situations can be seen as shocking or humiliating, and others as flattering or honourable, and that certain responses can be considered as appropriate and others as inappropriate – whether it be to fight or flee, to welcome or reject, to submit or protest, to forgive or avenge. To have any stability in our lives we have to try to organise these perceptions and responses into a fairly consistent, or 'constant', pattern which is suited to the sort of persons we want to be. ('Set' and 'constancy' are the psychologists' technical words.)

behaviour where neither law nor religion – nor even custom – *dictates* which choice is to be made. If we ask ourselves what influences us in these situations we might well find that we have developed attitudes about conduct which are derived unsystematically from many cultural sources. These could include formal moral teaching as well as ideas we have picked up from our reading of poetry, history or fiction, from films and television programmes, and from the examples set by our 'heroes', whether they be Che Guevara, Georgie Best, Jimi Hendrix, Mahatma Gandhi or Winston Churchill. But behind these, affecting the way we see and choose our heroes, and the way artists and writers see and choose themes, are the myths of our civilisation, whether Christian or pagan.

Myth in the Hellenistic World and in Imperial Rome

During the fifth and fourth centuries BC, when the myths were still believed by most Greeks, they were powerfully effective for conveying (as in Attic tragedy) religious and moral ideas. After the fourth century, with the decline of the city-state as the focus of social and political loyalties, religious interest in the Olympian gods began to wane and was transferred to the worship of local gods and heroes, or to religions which came from the east, such as those of Cybele, Isis and Mithras (and, eventually, Christianity). Among the sophisticated upper classes there was a growing indifference to religion altogether, and a greater attraction towards the teaching of philosophers. (This is not to say that they became atheists: they still believed that there were gods but ceased to take the traditional myths and the traditional worship seriously.) These developments first took place among the Greeks living under the rulers who succeeded Alexander the Great, and later at Rome in the last century before the birth of Christ. The philosophers either disregarded the old legends in their teaching, or taught that the old stories about the gods, even those that were blatantly immoral by the standards of the times, were really allegories or parables containing great wisdom and truth, which they proceeded to interpret.

Meanwhile literature and art continued to be preoccupied with mythological matter. Mythological allusions became a sort of literary furniture, valuable for comparisons and contrasts, rich in associations with masterpieces of classical literature and art. The stories lent themselves to frivolous or lightly romantic treatment (the Roman poet Ovid excelled at this). More serious poets used them to give dignity and universality to worldly themes. For instance, the stories of Jason and Medea and of Aeneas and Dido gave scope to acute psychological studies of women sacrificing duty to passionate love, and, in the case of Aeneas, of a man sacrificing love to duty.[1] Religious themes could still be treated mythologically; notably in the Sixth Book of Virgil's *Aeneid*; but there the mythical Underworld is charged with new symbolic meaning derived from philosophy as much as from religious thought and far removed from the Underworld of the *Odyssey*.

Pagan Myths and Early Christianity

One might have supposed that the triumph of Christianity would sweep the pagan gods and heroes into oblivion, but this was not so at all. At first, during the years when Christianity and paganism were fighting for the soul of the Roman Empire, the Christian leaders portrayed the pagan gods as evil demons. When Christianity was victorious the Christian authorities were unwilling to abolish the traditional education based on the great classical authors, even though their works were full of pagan mythology. Their continued study was indeed denounced by some churchmen, but to little effect. Others interpreted the stories of gods and heroes as edifying allegories,[2] just as the Hellenistic philosophers had done, and this justification for the study of pagan mythology was revived again and again through the centuries whenever it was attacked by the pious as a wicked pastime.

The Pagan Myths in the Middle Ages

Thus the gods survived into the Middle Ages both as demons and as allegorical figures. In a medieval account of St Benedict the story was told that when he was near Monte Cassino, preaching against idolatry, he converted a temple of Apollo into a Christian chapel; but the god revenged himself by tormenting St Benedict in the shape of a black monster with flaming eyes. And in the *Song of Roland* the Saracens pray to Mahound (Mohammed), to a mysterious deity called Termagant, and to Apollin, who is none other than the god Apollo, halfway through his transformation into the foul fiend Apollyon who nearly destroyed the soul of Christian in the Valley of Humiliation in Bunyan's *Pilgrim's Progress*.

On the other hand interpretations such as that which made the story of Leda and the Swan into an allegory of the alliance of Power and Injustice resulting in Scandal and Immorality (that is, Helen of Troy) found much favour with some medieval churchmen; and many of them claimed to discover profound moral truths in the witty and frivolous stories of Ovid.

---

[1] See *Aeneas and the Roman Hero* in this series.

[2] For instance the story of Kronos devouring his offspring was interpreted as being another way of saying that Time destroys everything it creates.

As for the legends, the story of Troy was no less popular than the stories of King Arthur as the subject for knightly romance, and scholars found mythical ancestors from among the heroes of Troy for most of the peoples of Europe.

A medieval interpretation of the abduction of Persephone (Preserpine in the picture) by Hades (Pluto). Persephone, with her bunch of flowers, is about to be dragged into the chariot (or wagon). A half-human Kerberos (Cerberus), armed with a spiked club, acts as Pluto's bodyguard

The Renaissance and after

In the ancient world the appearance of the gods and goddesses had been fixed descriptively by the poems of Homer and Hesiod, and in visible form by the great sculptors and painters of the classical age. In the Dark and Middle Ages the sculptures and paintings were mostly destroyed or buried, and the pagan gods took on, in medieval paintings, new shapes and attires to accommodate them to the familiar sights of the medieval world. When the Renaissance princes, merchants, scholars and artists started to uncover and study what had been buried or gone unnoticed for centuries, the gods began to appear again, in the art of fifteenth-century Italy and after, in their full classical splendour. And such they have remained ever since, vehicles for the symbolic and allegorical expression of innumerable ideas and ideals. To mention just two very different examples: Shelley used the myth of Prometheus to express his hatred of authoritarianism and cruelty, while the German philosopher Nietzsche seventy years later revived the concept of the god Dionysos to express his passionate belief in will to power and joy in life, and his hatred of Christian humility and self-abnegation.

The Modern World

Nor are the myths dead in our own century. One of the most terrible experiences that any generation has had to undergo was that suffered by the French when in 1940 their country was overrun and occupied by a ruthless enemy who set out to crush without mercy the attempts of patriotic Frenchmen to build up a network of resistance. All Frenchmen faced the agonising dilemma: was it right to engage in an apparently hopeless conspiracy of violence to resist their conquerors; or was it better to acquiesce and make the best of a bad situation by collaborating with the enemy. This problem was treated by Jean Anouilh in a play which told the legend of Antigone as a conflict between defiant idealism and intelligent realism.

The fear-haunted lives of the members of the Resistance, men and women whose organisations were, in the words of a French historian, 'a sort of Penelope's web, continually unpicked by the Gestapo, of which the bloody threads were obstinately re-knotted night after night', were re-created by Jean Cocteau in a film about Orpheus and Eurydike, in which the Underworld appears gruesomely like the cellars of a bomb-ravaged city, code messages from the Underworld are transmitted by radio in cryptic phrases like those which the BBC used to broadcast to the Resistance agents, and the henchmen of Death wear black uniforms grimly reminiscent of those of the Gestapo officials who manned the torture chambers and concentration camps where so many of the members of the Resistance ended their lives.

What was the value of treating this experience in the form of myth? Poetry, said the philosopher Aristotle, is more serious and significant than history because history is about particular things, whereas poetry is about universal things: and by poetry he meant the poetry of Homer and the Attic tragedians, which is entirely concerned with myths and legends. Perhaps the association of the events of 1940–5 with myths which reach far back into the past of our civilization, and – if Freud and Jung are right – deep into our Unconscious, helped the survivors of those events to accept the evil cruelty of torturers and executioners, the selfishness and treachery of collaborators and the unrewarded heroism and sufferings of the dead, and to go on living in a world where such things could happen.

Peleus and Thetis again

THE PORTLAND VASE

We have some visual evidence, especially from sarcophagi, of the symbolic significance which myths could acquire for the sophisticated society of Imperial Rome. One such piece of evidence is the Portland Vase, a very celebrated possession of the British Museum. This vase is something of a mystery. The experts date it, on technical grounds, to the time of

A panoramic diagram of the decoration on the Portland Vase

A   B   C   D   E

Augustus, or shortly after, and consider that it must have been commissioned either as a wedding gift, or as a funeral urn, intended for some very distinguished person. The scene depicted on it is clearly mythological and symbolic, but it is not certain exactly whom all the figures represent. The most recent and convincing explanation is that it tells the story of Peleus and Thetis and its sequel. One side of the vase shows the courtship of Peleus and Thetis, and the other the immortality of Achilles and Helen. Peleus (*A*) enters by a gate into the kingdom of the sea which is presided over by Okeanos – the grandfather of Thetis, the source of life and the route to the realm of the dead. His head appears at the base of the vase's handles (*E* and *I*). Eros (*B*), who holds a marriage torch as well as his bow, guides Peleus to Thetis (*C*), beside whom, or from whom, appears a small sea-serpent which indicates her ability to change her shape (though evidently the artist is depicting a version of the myth in which the courtship was welcomed and not resisted). Poseidon (*D*), Lord of the Sea and one of Thetis' divine lovers, watches the scene with calm resignation.

The other side of the vase shows Achilles (*F*) on the White Island with Helen of Troy (*G*). Aphrodite (*H*), the Goddess of Love and instigator of the whole cycle of events, majestically surveys her handiwork.

The vase, if the experts are right, is contemporary with Virgil's *Aeneid*, a time when elaborately symbolical use was being made of myth to convey – as in Book VI of the *Aeneid* – ideas about life and death. It is possible, if not probable, that this vase was intended to hold the ashes of some very distinguished person, and bore a message of consolation for his family and of hope for the immortality of his soul.

F   G   H   I

The Portland Vase exemplifies a very sophisticated use of myth to meditate on death and immortality. Let us now glance at a very primitive myth of creation.

We have hitherto not drawn attention to a puzzling aspect of the place of Thetis in Greek mythology. She is by birth merely one of the fifty delightful but seemingly unimportant daughters of Nereus, and yet she plays a very important role in the stories of the Olympian gods. A possible clue to this puzzle is provided by a surviving fragment from a lost poem by Alcman, who lived at the end of the seventh century BC, about fifty years after Hesiod. His creation myth, to judge from this fragment, was quite different from Hesiod's. In Alcman's myth it is Thetis who creates the world, with the help of three mysterious powers called Skotos (Darkness), Poros (Way) and Tekmor (a name which has no obvious meaning). Together they call the sun forth from the waters and bring order out of chaos. One scholar who has worked on this fragment thinks that there is an important religious significance in Thetis' connection with the cuttlefish, and in the contrast between the white meat it provides for food and the inky darkness of the fluid it squirts out to avoid capture. If this analysis is correct, it suggests an origin for the myth going far back to a primitive state of society; and in any case it shows that Thetis had at one time a mythological importance independent of the males in her story; that is to say, she was a powerful and creative divinity in her own right, and not merely the daughter of Nereus, the beloved of Zeus and Poseidon, the wife of Peleus and the mother of Achilles.

Conclusion

We began with a beautiful sea-goddess riding on a dolphin towards the shore of Cape Sepias, to the arms of her mortal lover. We conclude with a cuttlefish, an odd and ugly creature, and its ability to create obscurity and confusion. Perhaps that too is symbolic.

Appendixes

A Cretan octopus

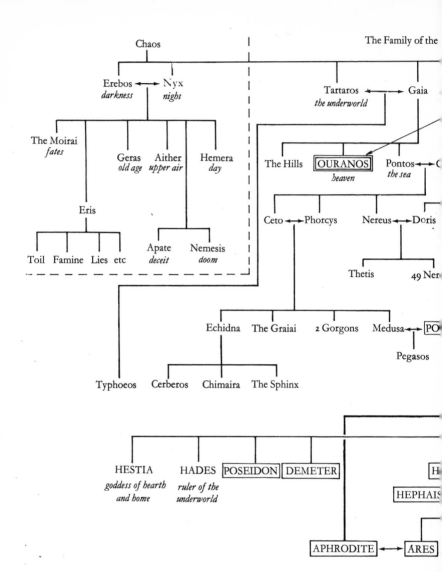

Chaos — The Family of the

Erebos *darkness* ←→ Nyx *night*   Tartaros *the underworld* ←→ Gaia

The Moirai *fates*   Geras *old age*   Aither *upper air*   Hemera *day*   The Hills   OURANOS *heaven*   Pontos *the sea*

Eris   Ceto ←→ Phorcys   Nereus ←→ Doris

Toil Famine Lies etc   Apate *deceit*   Nemesis *doom*   Thetis   49 Ner

Echidna   The Graiai   2 Gorgons   Medusa ←→ PO

Pegasos

Typhoeos   Cerberos   Chimaira   The Sphinx

HESTIA *goddess of hearth and home*   HADES *ruler of the underworld*   POSEIDON   DEMETER   H

HEPHAIS

APHRODITE ←→ ARES

Eros
*the sex instinct
(without which there would
have been no procreation)*

OURANOS

os ←→ Tethys Titans (Hyperion, Iapetos and others) 50-headed Giants Rheia ←→ **KRONOS**

yx Metis
*ver of the wisdom
world*

Atlas Prometheus Epimetheus ←→ Pandora

Deukalion ←→ Pyrrha
alone of mortals | survived the flood

Hellen

The Hellenes
the Greeks

ZEUS ←→ Metis
ATHENA

ZEUS ←→ **DEMETER**
Persephone

ZEUS ←→ Mnemosyne *(Memory)*
The 9 Muses

ZEUS ←→ Leto
TEMIS **APOLLO**

ZEUS ←→ Maia
HERMES

ZEUS ←→ Semele
DIONYSOS

☐ indicates supreme ruler

☐ indicates one of the
twelve Olympians

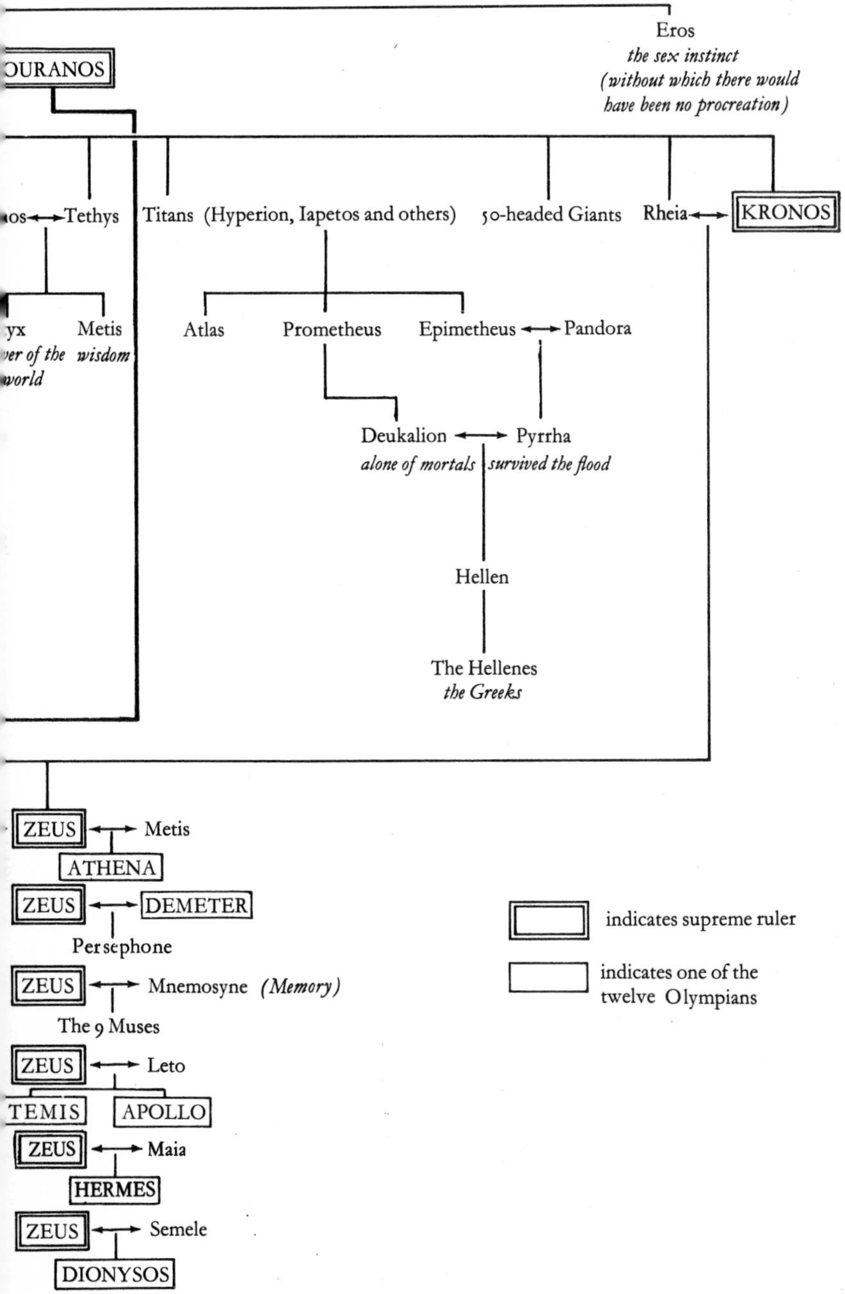

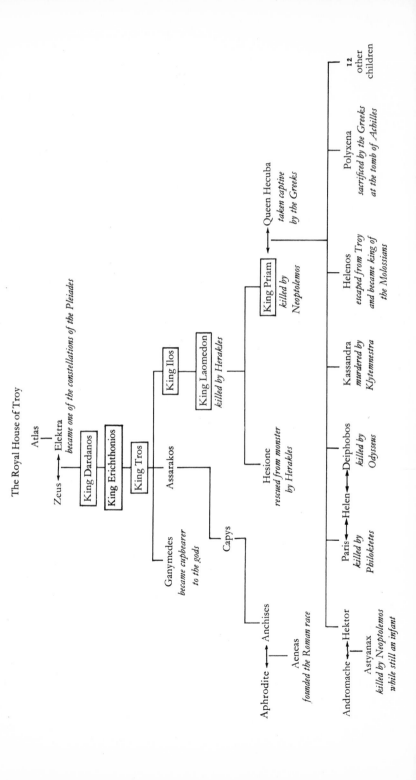

The Royal House of Troy

Zeus ⟷ Elektra
became one of the constellations of the Pleiades

Atlas

King Dardanos

King Erichthonios

King Tros

Ganymedes
became cupbearer to the gods

Assarakos

King Ilos

King Laomedon
killed by Herakles

Hesione
rescued from monster by Herakles

Capys

Anchises ⟷ Aphrodite

Aeneas
founded the Roman race

King Priam ⟷ Queen Hecuba
killed by Neoptolemos | *taken captive by the Greeks*

Paris ⟷ Helen ⟷ Deiphobos
killed by Philoktetes | *killed by Odysseus*

Kassandra
murdered by Klytemnestra

Helenos
escaped from Troy and became king of the Molossians

Polyxena
sacrificed by the Greeks at the tomb of Achilles

12 other children

Hektor ⟷ Andromache

Astyanax
killed by Neoptolemos while still an infant

The Rulers of Thebes and their relations

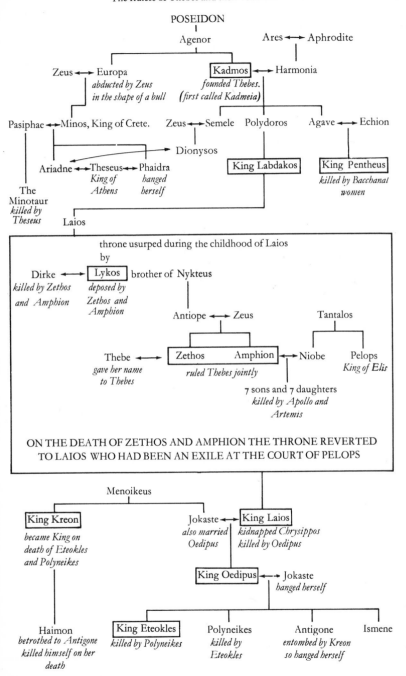

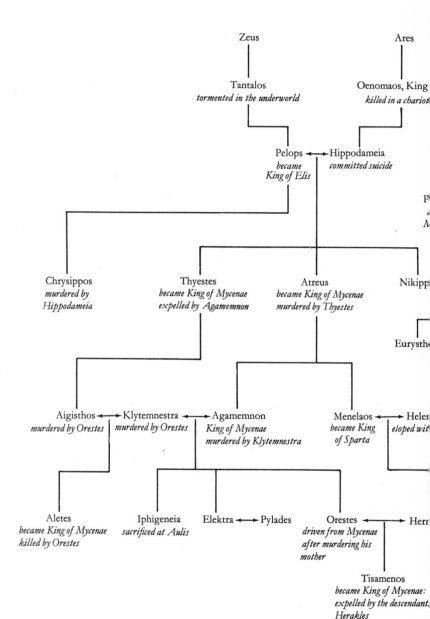

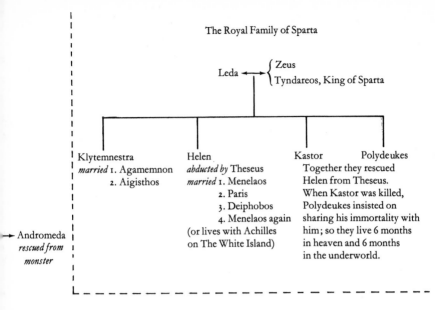

The Royal Family of Sparta

Leda ←→ { Zeus
Tyndareos, King of Sparta }

Klytemnestra
married 1. Agamemnon
2. Aigisthos

Helen
abducted by Theseus
married 1. Menelaos
2. Paris
3. Deiphobos
4. Menelaos again
(or lives with Achilles
on The White Island)

Kastor   **Polydeukes**
Together they rescued
Helen from Theseus.
When Kastor was killed,
Polydeukes insisted on
sharing his immortality with
him; so they live 6 months
in heaven and 6 months
in the underworld.

Andromeda
*rescued from
monster*

thenelos
ing of Mycenae

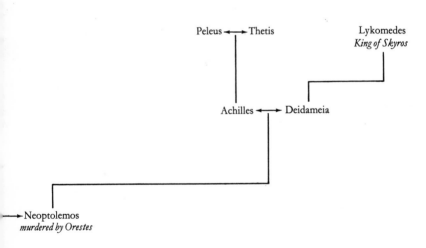

Peleus ←→ Thetis

Lykomedes
King of Skyros

Achilles ←→ Deidameia

Neoptolemos
murdered by Orestes

THE MAPS

1. *Opposite*: Greece, the islands of the Aegean sea and the coast of Asia Minor, showing places mentioned in the text.

2. *Below opposite*: Northern Central Greece, showing the site of the wooing of Thetis, and of the shipwreck of Xerxes' armada.

3. *Below*: Southern Greece (the Peloponnese), the Isthmus of Corinth, and Attica, showing places mentioned in the stories of the Tantalids and of Theseus.

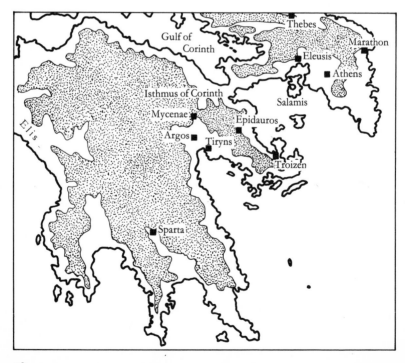

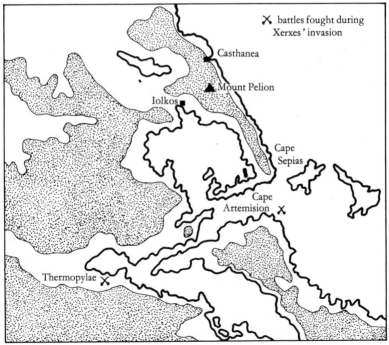

Index

OF NAMES OF GREEK GODS AND GODDESSES, HEROES AND HEROINES

It is impossible to know precisely how the Greeks pronounced the names of their gods and heroes, and even if it were possible no English-speaking person could imitate the sounds accurately without long practice. In preparing this index the author has received valuable advice from C. W. Baty, but he has not taken it all, and the mistakes are his own.

* Indicates where the familiar non-Greek spelling or pronunciation has been kept. Stressed syllables are underlined. Heavy type numerals refer to genealogies.

Another Cretan octopus